THE OUTFIELDER

How the dreadful secrets and lies of an Auschwitz
death camp survivor almost destroyed his
American-born son, the outfielder that never was

By
Carl L. Steinhouse
and
Joseph A. Richman

Based on the screenplay, *The Outfielder*, by Joseph A. Richman

authorHOUSE®

AuthorHouse™
1663 Liberty Drive
Bloomington, IN 47403
www.authorhouse.com
Phone: 1-800-839-8640

First published by AuthorHouse 10/31/2011

ISBN: 978-1-4670-6643-3 (e)
ISBN: 978-1-4670-6644-0 (sc)

Library of Congress Control Number: 2011918633

Printed in the United States of America

Any people depicted in stock imagery provided by Thinkstock are models, and such images are being used for illustrative purposes only. Certain stock imagery © Thinkstock.

This book is printed on acid-free paper.

"You know very well, Bernie, that your father gave you no choice but to become a doctor. And you had to be the best. As a result, you didn't follow your dreams. If you had, you might have played center field for the New York Yankees and had your plaque up on the wall at Cooperstown. You are the outfielder that never was."

THE OUTFIELDER

Prologue

'Tis the season. A peaceful snowy evening of contentment during the holidays–a contentment that swiftly turns into one of unspeakable horror and bloodshed.

Friday night, the second day of Christmas, and the Feldenstein family sits down to dinner, but not to celebrate the birth of Jesus, but to welcome the Jewish Sabbath, which they call *Shabbos*. They participate in this ritual on the eve of *Shabbos* as they do every week throughout the year. From sundown on Friday to sundown on Saturday, work stops to honor the Creator who, according to Genesis, rested on the seventh day of the creation of the world. While much of the world does rest on some seventh day, there are many believers who also celebrate the Sabbath for its reverence, for the Fourth of the Ten Commandments not only commands us to do no work on this day but to keep it holy. Despite its frequency, occurring every week throughout the year, religious Jews consider each and every *Shabbos* as among the most sacred of holidays.

Noah, 31, the eldest Feldenstein child, when he can, joins his parents and his sister Leah for the Friday night dinners. Despite the dangers of displaying any forms of Jewishness in Nazi Germany, he tries to respect his parent's traditions, the Sabbath eve meal included. And it is not unusual for his parents, again following

Hebrew tradition, to invite a guest to share their *Shabbos* dinner. Tonight is no exception.

As the aromas waft across the dining room–the freshly baked *challeh* (the twisted loaf of bread), the soup, and the roasted chicken–Mama Feldenstein initiates the meal by lighting the candles welcoming *Shabbos*. She covers her head, closes her eyes, and recites the blessings. Papa Feldenstein waits for her to finish before reciting the Kiddish declaring this day holy, and then intoning the blessings over the bread and wine. But before Mama could finish the candle lighting, a discordant melody intrudes on this pacific scene in the nature of a somewhat raucous chorus of *Silent Night* coming from outside in the front of their house, clearly heard despite the windows shut tight against the bitter winter cold.

Mama hesitates, looking up.

"Ignore them, Mama, they'll move on shortly," Papa says.

Papa Feldenstein is wrong. A loud insistent knocking on the door further intrudes on their ritual.

Papa pulls aside the curtains slightly and peers out the window. "There's a lot of uniformed Hitler Youths out there, fifteen or twenty of them, and they all look drunk."

"What's the matter, Jews," the family hears shouted through the closed front door, "don't you want to honor our Lord Jesus Christ while we serenade you?"

"Papa, *please* don't open the door," Noah pleads.

Papa shrugs. "They will only break it down, so let's be compliant and listen to the goyim serenade us."

"Please Papa, I know those Hitler Youths. They're out for blood, not to entertain."

The knocking grows louder and more threatening. The front window shatters from a rock hurled through it. Before anyone can restrain him, Papa rushes out the door, yelling, "Get the hell out of here, you criminal hoodlums."

A rock-laced snowball hits Papa over the left eye, leaving a bloody gash. He collapses into the snow. Immediately the youths are on him beating him with clubs and knives. He has no chance.

Leah and Mama rush outside to aid Papa. "Don't go out there," Noah screams. But they disappear outside. *I cannot do anything more, there are too many of them,* he thinks in desperation. *God, how can I leave them like this!*

"We must leave! We can go through the back window," Noah cries in anguish to his guest. "They won't find us in the woods."

"No, I'll stay, you go," his guest whispers, "I don't think they'll bother me."

Noah, wild-eyed and not prone to argue, climbs out a rear window, disappearing into the dark forest.

While Jews are expendable, the boys of the Hitler Youths are not. Gestapo officers arriving on the scene ignore the Hitler Youths as they step carefully around the body of Papa, certainly not out of respect but simply to avoid sullying with his blood, their highly shined black boots. They set out to find Noah Feldenstein.

Auschwitz Concentration Camp, Circa 1943

Noah Feldenstein stands at the railroad siding just inside the main gates of the Auschwitz Concentration Camp, stamping his feet in the frigid wet weather of this February day. His shoes, with more holes than soles, offer little protection from both the cold and the dampness. Finally, he hears the train whistle and looks down the tracks. The single bright headlight of the locomotive in the distance cuts through the air, unconcerned with the dismal weather.

A German officer approaches. "Ah, Herr Doctor, another trainload of Jews approaches. You know the procedure; all those you deem healthy and strong enough for labor will be motioned to the right side of the platform, the rest will move to the left side for disposition."

Feldenstein doesn't need instructions. He knows damn well what "the rest" means: the elderly, the infirm, most of the women, and all of the children, except for twins, of course, who will be segregated from those destined for immediate disposition. And "disposition" is simply a convenient euphemism for extermination. Auschwitz is not only a concentration camp, its connected Birkenau sector is also a death camp. A train usually brings in a few thousand Jews at once, so Feldenstein is one of many Jewish doctors performing this grisly sorting operation this cold night.

Feldenstein shakes his head. *The poor bastards—they've been through hell being transported here in sealed cattle cars, their one-bucket of water-exhausted days ago, and their one tin chamber pot overflowing for days.*

Feldenstein feels the discomfort of the German officer's cold stare. "Be sure to withhold nothing from me. Understand?" Then his face softens into a smile. "I expect we will be keeping you and your colleagues busy next spring when we will be shipping in a few hundred thousand of your Hungarian brethren Jews."

Feldenstein simply looks down at his tattered shoes. He says nothing. The German officer really is not expecting a dialogue. Indeed, one wrong word or look could spell disaster for Feldenstein.

The officer steps up, his face close to Feldenstein's, so close, the inmate doctor could smell the German's bad breath. The officer slaps his riding crop against the side of his black boots. "Listen carefully, Jew. Do your job well or you will join your brethren in the gas chambers."

Feldenstein nods.

Feldenstein exchanges glances with another Jewish doctor standing further down the siding who, like Feldenstein, waits to begin the ghoulish task.

Feldenstein has the same haunting thoughts every time a new load of Jews arrives. Will this never end? These poor people, with their meager possessions, some with jewelry, some with food secreted in their pockets, all looking for some way to survive. And regardless of what I do, most won't. So what is the use?

The locomotive chugs far enough into the camp so that the last car clears the entrance and the heavy gates clang shut. The engineer applies the brakes. Each cattle car noisily slams into couplings of the car in front of it and, one after the other, they come to a jolting halt. Suddenly, chaos erupts. Powerful lights flood the train siding as German soldiers and Kapos–those inmates in striped pajamas assigned guard duties and often as cruel as their German masters– fling open the doors of the cattle cars. They shove ramps against the car sliding doors. Screams of "Raus! Raus! Out! Out! Schnell! Schnell!" permeate the scene as Jews, without water, food, or sanitary facilities for days, stumble out of the cars and down the ramps onto the siding. Kapos rip suitcases and other possessions out of their hands and load them on trucks, eventually to be sent to German civilians. Those who do not move fast enough are clubbed and left to die where they collapse. The Kapos then jump in the cars and toss out, like sacks of potatoes, the bodies of those who died in transit as inevitably, many do.

They might be the lucky ones, Feldenstein thinks.

Feldenstein has only seconds to make his decisions, quickly motioning the arrivals to one side of the siding or the other. Many push their possessions onto him. He has had to harden himself against the pleas, requests for food, anguish, and injuries of the arrivals–and the inevitable separation of families. *Suppress any feelings of sympathy or soon I will join them.* Down the line, other Jewish doctor inmates are making similar life and death decisions under the same duress, a far cry from what these physicians spent so many years training to be and to do. All the women and children are motioned to the left. Some of the women, the very healthy ones, are pulled out and sent to the right. All the elderly and infirm are motioned to the left. Those on the left will be transported immediately to the gas chambers for extermination; those on the right will be assigned to forced labor under extremely cruel conditions. Feldenstein is not sure which group is better off.

But what choice do the Jewish doctors have? Feldenstein reasons to himself. The doctors are demoralized, undernourished, and overworked. Extreme deprivation and the human instinct for survival–these can do things to a person, change him into someone he never thought he could become–it could, in effect, make him into a killer instead of a healer. Of course, the Jewish doctors do minister to the sick in the labor camps, but without medicine, it is a near impossible task to treat simple general medical problems, much less the typhoid, hunger, edema, dysentery, and tuberculosis that they see every day. Vermin, lice, and boils cover patients in the wards. Occasionally, we could lay our hands on a few aspirins–that plus some reassuring words is the extent of our treatment. Sometimes it did wonders, but the doctors often end up dealing with ungrateful patients, patients who feel that at least one of doctors at the clinic had fingered some of their relatives for extermination.

And then there was the human medical experimentation on the inmates, particularly twins, and the Nazi doctor, Joseph Mengele, whom they called the "Angel of Death". . . Feldenstein pushes the thought out of his mind; he cannot deal with it.

Chapter 1

Psychiatrist Dr. Bernard Feld leans back in the plush leather desk chair in his Manhattan office just off Central Park. He looks at his watch–just a few minutes before his next patient. Reaching over to his credenza, he picks up a well-worn baseball glove and pounds its pocket with his fist. He loves the smell of the leather and the oil worked into it–done to keep the pocket soft and supple. He sighs and closes his eyes. As usual, when he picks up the glove, he begins yet again to think about his early years in Brooklyn . . .

* * *

Yankee fans are rare for this neighborhood, but nevertheless there they were, on his Brooklyn sidewalk, a few boys ranging from ten to twelve years old. They are huddled nervously over a tinny-sounding transistor radio. I am twelve and no lover of the Yankees. I stand off to the side also listening intently. The noise of the broadcast of the 1960 World Series wafts through the open window of a first floor apartment of a tenement building in the Brooklyn. There is plenty of static, but the play-by-play report is still understandable. "Come on, Terry, strike him out," one of the Yankees fans pleads fervently to the radio, as if his voice in Brooklyn could urge on Yankee pitcher Bill Terry at the Pittsburgh Pirate's Forbes Field. I root just as fervently for a hit, but silently.

"Mazeroski hits a long drive to left field, Berra races back; he can't get it; it's over the left field wall; it's over the wall for a home run! The Pittsburgh Pirates win the 1960 World Series, four games to three; the Pirates win the World Series!"

A kid angrily flips off the radio and points. "Look at him with that big smile on his face. The lousy Yankee hater, let's get 'em and wipe that grin off his puss."

The noise of the yelling and cursing filters into a ground- floor apartment.

"He's hurt. Let's get the hell out of here."

* * *

Bernie Feld does not say a word. He just sits there, scruffy and dirty, facing his father, Noah Feld, who slowly and deliberately moves back and forth in his rocking chair, staring at his son. Bernie hates these silences; he avoids looking at his father, letting his eyes wander around the modestly decorated living room—modest except for the large and ornate breakfront dominating one wall with religious items displayed on its shelves. He could see a Kiddush cup, a menorah, a spice box, and silver—not silver-plate, mind you—candlestick holders the family uses on the eve of Shabbos. If his father expects Bernie to speak first, he'll have a long wait. The front door opens and Bernie's mom, carrying several packages, kicks the door closed behind her. She looks at Bernie who jumps up and runs to his bedroom slamming the door. Through the closed door, he could hear his parents arguing in the living room. He sat on the floor pounding the baseball into his glove. He wishes he couldn't hear them. The arguing stops.

A light taping on the door and his mother enters.

"Just look at you Bernie, you're nose is bleeding. Are you okay?"

"Where were you, Mom? I needed you."

"Don't be too harsh on your father. You have to understand; he has been through so very much pain that we can never hope to begin to understand."

Bernie looks up at her, his eyes moist. And not from his bloody nose. "I heard what you said to Dad downstairs. You're going away, aren't you, Mom?"

"Just for a week or two, dear. But I'll be back. I am going to Germany and perhaps Israel. I have saved for a year for this trip. If you weren't in school, I would bring you along."

"No, you won't return," he said petulantly. "You're never coming back."

"Don't worry dear, I will be back. And do you want to know why? Because you're here."

Bernie looks doubtful. "You promise?"

She sighs. "I promise, Bernie."

"Miriam, you must come downstairs and let the boy study," the father calls out.

"You really promise?" Bernie presses.

"I promise." She takes a baseball out of her apron pocket. She flips it to him. "It's brand new." She leans down, kisses her son on the forehead, and leaves the room, closing the door gently behind her.

Chapter 2

The incessant buzz of his intercom struggles to get his attention, but the doctor seems oblivious; or perhaps he just plain ignores the intrusive sound. A knock on his office door finally rouses Dr. Bernard Feld out of his reverie. His father's photo hangs on the wall behind him–the only family photo in his office.

The door opens slowly and cautiously; his secretary Arlene, sticks her head in. "Dr. Feld, are you all right? Sorry to disturb you but your next patient, Dyan Regan, is here for her appointment."

Dr. Feld yawns and stretches. "Sorry, Arlene, I wasn't ignoring you. I must have dozed off. Please send Ms. Regan in."

Arlene rolls her eyes, sighs, and leaves to fetch Ms. Regan.

Dr. Feld leans back in his chair. His tastefully decorated, if somewhat lavish, office has the typical framed medical degrees and licenses displayed prominently on the walls and the not-so-typical–at least for a psychiatrist–collection of baseball memorabilia and photos of Brooklyn Dodger players posing at Ebbets Field, where they used to play.

As Dyan Regan, an attractive brunette in her late thirties enters, Dr. Feld stands to greet her, but she ignores him; instead she walks across the office to his bookshelf, searching. She pulls out one book, holds it up, and faces Feld.

"Freud? Is that what I am, one of your experiments?"

Feld ignores her barb. "Hello, Dyan. How are you?"

"Fine, I suppose." Regan sighs.

Feld looks at her with concern.

Regan frowns. "For crying out loud, stop staring at me."

Feld shrugs. "Sorry if I'm making you feel uncomfortable."

She places her hands on his desk, leaning forward provocatively, displaying some cleavage that disappears down into her blouse. A small smile crosses her face. "Bet'cha don't know where I spent the weekend."

"Why don't you sit down on the couch and make yourself comfortable? Then you can tell me."

Regan flops onto the deep leather couch. "Beekman Memorial Hospital, that's where I was all weekend. Had another damn asthma attack on the subway platform and collapsed onto the tracks. It took a cop and two token collectors to lift me to safety."

Feld rubs his chin, studying his patient. "Now Dyan, didn't I send you to that specialist, Dr. Willis, and didn't he give you asthma medicine for your condition? You assured me that you were taking the medicine."

"Yeah, well–you know doctor, that until I started seeing you, the last time I had had an attack was when I was ten years old. Damn it, I came to you to move forward with my life, not backwards."

Feld frowns. "How was I to know you had stopped taking your asthma medicine? Dyan, I specifically discussed with you that I was rather concerned that the stress of therapy might trigger an attack. That's why I referred you to Dr. Willis in the first place. Remember?"

"Oh, come on, Dr. Feld, I know what you are doing–trying to bond with me. But aren't you laying it on rather thick with that 'rather concerned' line?"

Feld shakes his head slowly. "It's no line, I assure you. It's just that you are not accustomed to anyone showing concern for you."

Regan glares at him. "What did you expect, Mr. Expert? After all,

I was brought up in four different foster homes–count 'em–four. Who could stay around long enough for anyone to show concern? And, God forbid, if I slipped up, I was sent back to boarding school."

Feld sighs. "Boarding school, you say? Don't you mean orphanage? Dyan, in boarding school, parents pay for their children's upkeep and education. An orphanage is where parentless and abandoned children go."

Regan shrugs. "Okay, so it was an orphanage. But I'm not here to argue semantics, so why don't we just cut to the chase, shall we? Here's the bottom line. I want to keep my little boy and will do everything I must to keep him. Is that clear enough for you? Does your *concern* extend far enough for you to help me keep my son?"

Feld strokes his chin. "Well, I won't let you fall in front of another subway train, but I will help you resolve your inner conflicts–and denial. And that's how I can assist you and your son."

"I guess my whole life has been a lie, huh?"

Feld smiles. "Ah, honesty, the first step towards resolving your problems. You will get there, Dyan. And I will help. But first, we need to get to the truth by dealing with your anger, grief, and sorrow; it's a necessary part of this process. Eventually, all those emotions will fall away, you'll see. Having no parents is the reality of your past. But now you have a need to protect your mother by saying she sent you to boarding school. In fact, you had no mother and you grew up in an orphanage and various foster homes."

Regan jumps up and starts to pace around the room. She pointed an accusing finger at him. "Look, I know you're trying to help, but I'm not one of your little Freudian monkeys."

Feld shakes his head. "Harlow."

She looks at him, her brow furrowed. "What?"

"It was Harlow that experimented with monkeys, not Freud. Harlow took three groups of new-born monkeys; he put one group with real mothers, another group with padded-doll mothers, and the third group he gave mothers made of wire."

Regan rolls her eyes. She jumps up, defiant, with hands on her hips. "So?"

"So–the monkeys with the real mothers were normal; the monkeys with the padded dolls were neurotic; and those with wire mothers were almost psychotic. The point I'm making is that our first relationship is our most important–and that is usually our mother."

She plops down on the couch. "That takes care of my mommy. Yours must have been a wire mommy."

Her statement takes him by surprise. It shouldn't have, but it did. He searches for an answer. He thinks back to that day of the altercation with his father . . .

Chapter 3

Bernie Feld, now sixteen, feels satisfied with the workout at the high school baseball team practice. He hit quite a few over the fence while in the batting cage. He takes his usual shortcut home, jogging under the bleachers. This day it is a mistake. Four members of the team lie in wait for him. One-on-one, Feld could take pretty good care of himself, but today the odds were stacked against him when the four of them jumped him.

"Damn Jew bastard," the leader of the bunch shouts at Feld. "Trying to show us up, eh? I bet you paid the practice pitcher to lob those cream puff pitches in there so you could impress the coach. Let's teach the kike a lesson!"

Feld staggers back to the locker room. The baseball coach takes one look at him, bundles him into his car, and drives him to the emergency room.

* * *

Noah Feld puts down the newspaper and gets up to answer the door.
A man stands at the threshold. The elder Feld does not recognize him.
"Can I help you?"
"Dr. Feld?"
"Yes, that's me."
The stranger puts out his hand. "Hello, Dr. Feld, I'm Barry Levinson, your son's gym teacher."

Dr. Feld looks at Levinson quizzically and finally extends his own hand, but without enthusiasm.

"And what is the occasion for a visit from Bernie's teacher? Is he in trouble?"

Levinson shakes his head. "No, nothing like that. I came to see how your son was after that altercation at school."

"He's mending. It's not the first time he's gotten into fights with the Goyim—you know, the Gentiles."

Levinson nods. "Yes, I understand some Yiddish. I tried to get him to file a police report but he would not identify his attackers. He said he just fell down."

Dr. Feld shrugs. "Yes, I know, he can be very stubborn."

Levinson smiles. "Like most kids his age. But he'll heal and his life will go on."

"So, besides being a gym teacher, you are also here to teach me philosophy?"

Levinson shrugs.

Dr. Feld folds his arms across his chest. "If that's all, I have to start my afternoon prayers."

"Sorry. I'm also the high school baseball coach."

"Baseball? That's how my son received that beating—because of baseball."

"No, Dr. Feld, it wasn't because of baseball. The boys who assaulted him are troublemakers."

"You mean thugs, like the Hitler Youth and Storm Troopers. Are you a Jew, Mr. Levinson?"

Levinson nods.

"Well, let me tell you, I experienced such boys in Nazi Germany, under Hitler. They killed my father and sent my mother and sister to die in the death camps."

"I'm very sorry, Dr. Feld, truly I am."

"Well then, just why are you here, Mr. Levinson?"

"You know, Dr. Feld, your son is a very talented baseball player and when he graduates high school, I am fairly certain I can get him a scholarship to Tufts University, where I will be teaching this fall. It's a first-class learning institution."

Dr. Feld shakes his head. "So, mazel-tov."

"You must listen. Your son is one of the finest young athletes I've seen. He has a very special talent for baseball. If he continues to play I can guarantee him a full scholarship."

"Absolutely not. Baseball is for those Gentiles, the ones that beat him up simply because he is a Jew. He's better than those boys and I will see that he becomes a doctor, as I was in Germany—a doctor, Mr. Levinson, not a ballplayer. You understand me?"

"Dr. Feld, baseball and a medical career are not incompatible. He can play in college and still pursue his studies. I'll make sure it doesn't interfere with his studies."

"Baseball is not for Jewish boys."

"That's not so, Dr. Feld. Some of our greatest players were and are Jewish." He touched the fingers of his right hand one by one. "Hank Greenberg of Detroit, Al Rosen of Cleveland, Sandy Koufax of the Dodgers . . ."

Dr. Feld put up his hand, his lips pressed tight. "Enough, already! Bernie is going to concentrate on his studies and not be distracted by anything as trivial as baseball. I don't want you to continue filling his head with this baseball nonsense. His playing days on the team are over, finished.

"There is nothing more to discuss. Now if you will excuse me, I am already late for my prayers."

"Please, Dr. Feld. Have you considered that colleges, especially the elite ones, are very expensive? You'll need every penny that a scholarship can provide."

Dr. Feld sighs. "That is not your worry Mr. Levinson. The money will be there when my son needs it."

"I hope you will reconsider while there is still time."

"The only thing I will reconsider is whether to complain to the school authorities that you are interfering with my son's education."

Dr. Feld starts to close the door but Levinson is standing in the way.

"Mr. Levinson, do you keep the Sabbath?"

Levinson frowns. "I have my own relationship with God."

Dr. Feld nods. "I didn't think you did. Now please, step away from the door, it is time for prayers."

"Dad?"

Dr. Feld turns to see Bernie in the room.

"You heard, Bernie?"

"Yes and I am going to play baseball."

"Then you will live under someone else's roof, not mine."

"But I will become a doctor and still play ball, I promise you."

"You should have identified to the police the boys who beat you up."

"I fell, no one beat me up."

"Son, don't insult my intelligence."

Dr. Feld turns to the teacher. "Mr. Levinson, I appreciate your coming over, but if you don't mind, I would like to speak to my son—alone."

Levinson steps way from the threshold of the door. "Very well, have a good evening."

Dr. Feld shuts the door.

Dr. Feld sits down in his rocking chair. "Sit down, Bernie."

Bernie sits in a chair facing his father.

"You know that if boys get away with what they did to you, they will do terrible things later. I know, I saw it in Germany, son. Now, give me their names."

"No, I'll take care of this myself."

"Now what's this talk of taking care of things yourself? What are you? Some tough guy like you've seen in the movies? Is that how you've been brought up? You're no tough guy, Bernie."

"If you took the slightest interest in me you would have come out to watch me play. Then all of this wouldn't have happened."

"Now you blame me, Bernie? I might go to the park with you when I finish my work, but not to see you play baseball. I am disappointed you have been playing behind my back." Noah gets up, turns his back to Bernie, and looks out the window watching the descending darkness.

Bernie follows his father to the window. "Where's mom gone to? What happened to her? I could discuss things with mom."

Dr. Feld whirls around, staring angrily at his son. "You will talk to me! Your mother's never coming back. Face it, Bernie. They beat you up because you are a Jew."

"You weren't the only one in a concentration camp, you know. So get off that subject already."

Dr. Feld puts his face in Bernie's, glaring at his son. "Don't you dare speak to your father like that," he rages.

Bernie does not back down and Dr. Feld raises his open hand, prepared to strike him. He raises his eyes as if looking to heaven. "Oh, Lord, hold back my arm. Rip it from my body that I would use it to strike my only son." His arm goes slack.

Bernie backs away, a look of disbelief on his face.

Dr. Feld tone softens. "Bernie, those boys are like the ones under Hitler. The doctor at the hospital said you were lucky. They could have killed you."

"I'm still here, aren't I? Mr. Levinson says I'm really a good player."

"Are you listening to me, Bernie? You played baseball, you were on the team. I didn't know, but that's fine. But now, there will be no more baseball. Is that clear?"

"Mr. Levinson wants me to stay on the team—and I intend to."

"You would defy me, your father?"

Bernie glares back at his father.

Dr. Feld stalks out of the room, leaving Bernie standing there. He returns a few moments later with some of Bernie's things, throwing them at his son's feet. "You dare disobey your father? Then you are disobeying God. So, take your things and go. Play baseball; go find your Mr. Levinson. Perhaps you'll end up like him—a gym teacher."

"I would be proud to emulate him."

"Enough of this foolishness! Either go back to your room and study or go out that door."

"Did you drive mom away too?"

Dr. Feld glares at Bernie. "I won't dignify that question with an answer."

Bernie picks up his things and heads to the door.

"Son, if you do go out, then to me you'll be as good as dead, and I will sit Shiva."

Bernie eyes his father defiantly and stamps out the door, slamming it behind him.

Dr. Feld could hear Bernie in the hallway outside the apartment cursing and crying in rage and frustration. Dr. Feld hears the door open. Bernie shuffled back in, looking thoroughly defeated.

Dr. Feld puts his arm around his son. "It's for the best, Bernie, believe me. You have made the correct choice. Some day you'll thank me for seeing that you put all your efforts into your studies. You should follow in my footsteps. All the sacrifices I made, after being a doctor in Europe were made so that you, my son, could go to the best college and medical school. I didn't spend the money to go medical school here, and therefore couldn't practice medicine in the United States. All so that I could afford your education."

Bernie stomps into his room and slams the door shut, kicking aside a baseball bat leaning against the wall and swiping a baseball cap and glove off his desk. He recalls his promise to his mother to obey his old man. Now he's sorry he made it.

Bernie sighs and retreats into his usual daydream. It's Ebbets Field, 1960. He's playing left field; he looks over and sees Duke Snider patrolling center field and Carl Furillo at the ready in right field. He could hear Red Barber on the radio in his calm southern drawl filling the airwaves to the Dodger fans on the edge of their chairs, "Folks, it comes down to these last pitches with the game riding on the bat of Willie Mays. Giants have two on, the winning run at second base. Can the Say-Hey Kid drive in the runs that will defeat the Dodgers? Strikeout King Sandy Koufax is on the mound. He stretches, here's the pitch; it's a hard sinking line drive to left field, Feld charges in . . ."

Chapter 4

"Dr. Feld?"

He shakes his head and looks at Regan. He smiles. "Sometimes I have to go back in time in my own mind. But in answer to your question, yes, I have had mother issues. I was twelve when my mother left and I never saw her again. My memories go back to when I was two or three. But you have no memories at all. We have to find out why."

Regan holds her head in her hands. "I just want to keep my son," she says so softly, forcing Feld to lean forward, straining to hear her. "I want him to have his mother."

"Me too, Dyan. There is nothing more I want than to have you keep your son."

She looks up. Her eyes meet Feld's. "Are you going to report this to the courts?"

"No, I won't bring it up–but only if you promise you'll take your medication just as it was prescribed."

She pauses and looks at the floor. "Thanks, doctor."

"Dyan, you talked about going backwards after coming here. There's a reason for that. Many buried memories are percolating to the surface. Undoubtedly, they are disturbing and that's what triggered your asthma attack."

"There's got to be a better way. I don't want to dig up any more childhood memories. Let's find another route to take."

Feld gets up and moves around to the couch, gently placing his hand on her shoulder. "Memories, Dyan, are like feelings. When you bury them, they are still alive. Sometimes, the only way to leave them truly behind, is dealing with them directly."

Regan looks up at Feld, shaking off his touch. She spreads her arms wide. "Psycho babble! Hocus-pocus! That's what this all is."

"Hocus-pocus? Dyan, if you're correct, why not just humor me and go along? What do you have to lose?"

"My son. I've got my little boy to lose and I don't have time to play games with you."

"These 'games', as you put it, are an important step back to mental health."

"So what's in this for you, anyway, Doctor?" her tone suspicious sounding. "Why have you been seeing me all this time without charging?"

In Family Court, Judge Halloran asked me to review several *pro bono* cases and I chose to take on yours and a few others." Feld reaches into his side pocket and hands her a letter. "Your husband is demanding immediate custody of Bobby, citing your current therapy."

"How?" she cries. "Does that prove I'm crazy?"

"He claims you are unfit."

"He's the one who's unfit. Do you know that he's a drunk and abusive? Doesn't that count for something, for crying out loud? I think the whole thing's a joke."

"Unfortunately, Dyan, the court is not laughing. Judge Halloran has ordered me to make a final determination within sixty days on your fitness as a parent. The time began running last Friday. We now have fifty-seven days left."

"So, doctor, it's up to you."

Feld shakes his head. "No, Dyan, it's up to you."

Regan jumps off the couch again and stands in front of Feld's desk. She points at him. "But you're the one who determines whether I keep my son or not."

"Look, Dyan, Judge Halloran is a fair and impartial man–even if you did run out of his court."

Regan crushes the court letter in her fists. "That's not fair. I had to pick up my son at school."

"The judge will listen to all sides. He'll hear your husband's point of view and arguments, and he'll seriously consider my recommendation. Now, just so there is no misunderstanding between us, what I tell the court will be determined by the progress you make; it will depend on you and no one else."

Regan sits down on the couch, staring at the floor, saying nothing, continuing to crush the court's letter.

"Are we on the same page, Dyan? I need to know. We have fifty-seven days."

"Well, you're writing the book, aren't you? What page are we on now?"

"First, give me back the letter before you destroy it."

She gets up, hands him the crumpled letter after attempting to smooth it out somewhat and resumes her seat on the couch.

"Well, doctor, what do you want to know?"

"Dyan, tell me again about your dream, the one about the monsters. You told me that some were in your room and some on the outside. Those outside monsters, where were they? In the street? In another room? Somewhere else? Try to remember, it's important."

Regan fidgets, crossing her legs, showing more thigh. "I can't remember," she sniffs.

"Let's go back. You said you were 'trapped'? "

She nods. "I couldn't move. Listen, you know all this. Why do you keep asking me?" Regan stands up and walks to the window, staring out. "You know Doctor Feld, I slept with my last therapist."

Feld sighs. "A big mistake."

"Why a mistake?"

"It breaks the trust between you and your doctor. In one form or other, the treatment ends–always does."

Regan walks away from the window and leans suggestively on Feld's desk. She smiles coyly. "Maybe, just maybe, it would be the start of something else."

"Yes it would. It would be the start of the process of losing your son, a setback in your therapy, and an increase in your feelings of guilt and shame."

"Well bless my l'il ole heart, doctor. I do declare, you'all are right again." Regan drops the bogus southern accent. "After my last doctor screwed me for six months, he decided to refer me to someone else, ending my therapy sessions with him. His diagnosis? He said I had to screw people in authority. Is that what you think, Doctor Feld?"

"He missed the mark totally. You're fortunate you are not seeing him anymore."

"Oh really? Why is that, *Doctor*?"

"Your problem is not screwing others, it's screwing yourself. You get involved with sadistic men, force your employers to fire you, and then you fight with the judge, the very person who will decide whether you can keep custody of your son–or not. Finally, you do everything to sabotage your own therapy. Now I ask you Dyan, isn't that nothing but screwing yourself? You've spent your life doing that."

Regan sits down again. "Yeah, yeah. I've heard this routine before and I know the finale."

"Dyan, look at me. You are carrying some terrible guilt from your childhood and you won't permit yourself to have anything that looks even remotely like happiness. The bottom line is that either you get your act together–and soon–or you'll destroy any chance of retaining custody of your son. That awful guilt you carry around won't let you enjoy any happiness."

Regan rises off the couch and goes to the table displaying some of his memorabilia. "Are you happy Doctor Feld? I've never seen a more depressing office." She picks up his old baseball glove with the ball nestled in the pocket and waves it in front of him. "Look at this smelly old glove and ball–and photos of dead baseball players all over the place. It's just like a baseball mausoleum!"

She puts down the glove and ball and looks at him. "I see you're wearing a wedding band. How come there are no photos of your wife and kids around?" Regan taps one of the photos on the wall behind him. "And this photo of Freud? It's got to go."

Feld says nothing.

"I feel like the old goat is looking right into me–gives me the absolute creeps."

"It's not Freud," Feld finally answers softly; "it's my father."

"A baseball player?"

"Not likely. He was a highly respected physician in Europe. He's about to be honored in Israel. This week is the anniversary of his death."

Regan shrugs. "Sorry, it's just with all that baseball stuff you have around, I just assumed . . ."

Feld gets up and removes the photo, placing it face down on the table behind his chair. "For your sessions, I'll just take the picture down."

"You really don't have to, doctor."

"I want you to feel comfortable in the office."

Regan goes to the door and puts her hand on the doorknob. "Look, Doctor Feld, I'm really sorry. I'll bring you a plant next time to brighten up your office."

Feld puts up his hand. "Please, don't leave yet, Dyan."

He writes something out on a slip of paper, walks over, and holds it out to her.

She doesn't take it at first. "Let me guess. A referral slip to yet another shrink. I'm fired."

He pushes it into her hand. She takes the paper, her hand lingering on his. The doctor withdraws his hand.

"No, Dyan, you're not fired. The paper is simply a request for

Dr. Willis to give you another asthma prescription. I'll see you next week."

He joins her at the door. She looks into his eyes. For a moment, nothing is said. She turns the doorknob. "I'm meeting Bobby in the park later for a picnic. Should I tell my son he has only fifty-seven days?" She leaves, closing the door firmly.

Feld sighs, fetches the photo of his father, and returns it to its position on the wall. He flops into his desk chair, opens the middle drawer, and examines the photos of his wife and children.

The intercom buzzer interrupts his thoughts. "Dr. Feld, it's your wife on line one."

He picks up. "Hi Susan, how are you? Two o'clock? That's fine, see you then."

Chapter 5

All the memories that his sessions with Dyan had evoked in him surprised Feld–his abandonment by his mother, notwithstanding her promises; his father's insistence that he give up baseball and pursue his medical studies to the exclusion of everything else. He picks up the baseball his mother had given him just before she'd left for good. He tosses the ball in the air and catches it. He wanders over to the window. The memories keep flooding back.

* * *

Dr. Feld made it clear that baseball was out of the question if Bernie desired his father's financial support throughout his college studies and post-graduate work. That particularly grated on the young man because the Columbia Lions had a fine baseball program that had produced a few major leaguers such as Lou Gehrig, Eddie Collins, and Bill Finley. God, how he loved baseball; how much he'd give to test his skills on a professional level or at least in college. But he could not go against his father, not after what the old man had been through during the war and how he had suffered. Not that his father ever talked about it. He was a survivor from Auschwitz, that's about all Bernie could get out of him. So, like it or not, he'd become a doctor. As it turned out, he was no slouch in academics. He applied successfully to Columbia College. Not so many years back, the College admitted very few

Jews. As difficult as it was getting into the College, it was even more daunting gaining admission to The Columbia University College of Physicians and Surgeons. P&S, as the students and faculty called it, took some 150 students a year out of the six or seven thousand applicants. Bernie was one of those 150 and graduated P&S with top honors–but no baseball.

He specialized in psychiatry. Perhaps it would help him better understand people, especially his father.

* * *

The buzz of the intercom jolts him. "Dr. Feld? Don't forget, you have a lunch appointment with your wife. I'm sure you don't want to keep her waiting."

As usual, Arlene was right on the money. The last thing he needs now is to keep Susan cooling her heels.

Chapter 6

Feld slams the cab door, races past the nodding doorman, and into the Tavern On The Green, an iconic restaurant on the lower west side of Central Park at Sixty-Fifth Street. He glances around the main room. Normally, each time he entered, he'd stand somewhat in awe of the huge structure; his favorite room being the glass enclosed one with its large see-through roof and hundreds of trees, plants, and bushes inside and out, sharing space with the diners. The rumors are it will be closing. That would be too bad. But right now, the restaurant was in full swing, and he was late and striving vainly to spot his wife.

The maître d' approached Feld. "Can I help you?"

"Yes, I'm Dr. Feld and I am supposed to meet my wife here. I'm sure she's already here."

The maître d' smiled. "Ah, yes, she asked me to be on the lookout for you. Please follow me."

He spotted Susan, a good-looking woman in her mid-forty's, sipping a bourbon and soda, no doubt. At the other setting on the table stood an empty martini glass with an olive along with an insulated martini container, undoubtedly containing a chilled martini with a hint of vermouth, just waiting to be poured.

"Hello, dear. Sorry I'm late." He bends over to kiss her. She offers him her cheek.

"Why am I not surprised? I knew you'd be too busy to get here on time, so I took the liberty of ordering a drink for you."

He sits down. "Thanks, dear. I ran a little late with a patient. Can I get you a refill on that drink?"

"I've already knocked down two. But sure, I'll have another."

Feld motions the waiter. "Another bourbon and soda for the lady."

"I must say, you're looking well, Susan."

"Why not? It's the air on the Cape."

Feld nodded. "So what did you do this summer?"

"Well, the kids came out twice. We went sailing. And I did lot of soul-searching and thinking."

Feld raised his eyebrows but did not pursue that last comment. "How are the children? And your mother and father?"

"Everyone's fine. They all send their love."

Feld nods. The waiter returns with Susan's drink while Feld pours himself a martini.

"I have some good news, Susan. I've been offered the head position at the Psychiatric Department at Columbia General. I've decided to accept it. I'm going to be meeting with Saul Edelman who heads the department now. He's retiring."

Susan smiled. "I'm happy for you, Bernie."

"You realize what that means? Susan, I'll be able to spend more time at home, more time with you and the kids. I've finally got a nine-to-five job and can limit seeing patients only to one, or perhaps, two evenings a week." He fills his martini glass to the brim. "To celebrate, I booked us on a cruise to Europe where we can relax and sort things out."

He reaches for her hand. She does not reciprocate.

"It won't work Bernie. Look, our summer separation was a good idea. It let me do plenty of deep thinking. Bernie, I want a divorce. I prefer it to be a no-contest affair to keep it out of the courts. Let's leave it up to our lawyers to work out a settlement." She reaches in her purse, extracts some documents, and hands them to Feld. "These are the divorce papers. Please sign these and get them to my attorney. The sooner the better."

Feld frowns, draining his martini glass. "I know we can work this out. You don't have to do this."

"I've already worked it out, Bernie."

"But with this new position, things will be different, I promise you."

Susan shakes her head slowly. "Different? Truly, I don't think so. All that'll be different is that you'll spend all your time in the hospital instead of at an office."

"Really, Susan, you'll find most successful men devote a lot of time to their work. It's not unusual."

"That may be true but that's not you. Devoting time to your work is one thing, burying yourself in it is another."

"Okay, I can see you're upset. So let's just put this divorce issue aside for a little while we tour Venice and Paris. Then, when we get back, things will be different. You'll see."

"We're not in your office, so save me your counseling crap. You really think I'll exercise my woman's prerogative and change my mind?"

Feld shrugged. "At least we can relax and have time to talk."

"I don't have time. I'm meeting Beth for some shopping and then flying back to Boston."

"Sorry if having a calm, civil discussion interferes with your plans to go to Bloomingdales. Do you really think I'll simply sign away thirty years of marriage just like that?"

"I served my purpose already, didn't I? After all, you married me because it would be good for your career. At least that's what you told me on our wedding night. Do you remember? Listen, you think I don't know that if it were up to you, you would have married that little button-nose wasp *shiksa* cheerleader, Catherine, but daddy would not allow it because she wasn't Jewish. Oh, I know all about that. Look, Bernie, this hasn't been easy for me. We agreed to let me spend the summer apart so each of us could think. Well, I have, and this is what I want."

"What agreement, Susan? You need two people to have one. All I know is you ran to the Cape with a cheery 'I'll see you in September.' Now you try to shove this divorce down my throat?"

"That's not true. Oh shit, I've tried to talk to you–I can't count how many times. But *you* were always too busy." By now, she was shouting at Feld.

Feld, looking around, puts his index finger to his lips. "Please Susan–some of these people are my patients. Keep your voice down."

Susan stands, looks around the restaurant. "Attention! If you are a patient of my husband you are privileged because he's been far more intimate with you than has been with me."

Feld sighs, gets up, and tosses his napkin on the table.

Susan glares at her husband. "You're not leaving."

"We'll talk again when you are in more control of yourself."

Susan sits and points to his chair. "Sit yourself down Bernie, or I'll show you and all of these self-absorbed asses in this restaurant just what 'out of control is.' "

Feld sits down. "There's a fellow over there that likes to dress up in his wife's clothing and go to the Rangers' games in the Garden. I think you've set back his therapy three years."

Susan glares at Feld. "That's not funny. You think this is easy for me? Throughout our marriage, all I've been is your shadow. You move, I move. You sit, I sit. You stand, I stand. Never have I felt a sense of my own boundaries."

"Ah, I see–'boundaries', you say. Well, I see you have been reading some pop psychology." He smiles. "So what's the name of the book? 'You're OK, he's screwed up?' "

"No, Bernie, not that book but the one *you* wrote called, 'Coming to Terms with Yourself.' Sound familiar?"

Feld leans forward. "Susan, you're frightened, that's why you are overreacting."

"You're damn well right I am frightened," she growled.

Feld sighs. "Have you met someone else?"

"Think I can't do this on my own? You don't get it, Bernie, you really don't."

"Then why don't you explain it to me? I'm listening."

"An explanation? How about twenty-seven years of loneliness and alienation of affection? You think putting an expensive diamond on my finger and saying 'I do' is sufficient? You never really married me."

"Whom did I marry?"

"Your patients and your success, that's whom you married."

"You've never complained about my success and our affluence–or loneliness."

"Oh, I sure did. Only you never heard me, Bernie. I was so damn lonely; I'd go down to the river at night and watch the ships. Did you ever count the number of lights on the Fifty-Ninth Street Bridge? You know, standing in the shadows, I once watched a woman jump off that bridge. I'd stroll along the East River and see the lovers on the benches and cry from remembering our first few years together." Susan dabbed her eyes with a handkerchief. "You recall when you were struggling to make ends meet and an evening out consisted of the daily special at the Coney Island Diner and one ride on the Wonder Wheel? You even sold your valuable picture of Babe Ruth in order to buy me a first anniversary present."

Feld shook his head. "Ty Cobb."

"What?"

"The picture I sold was of Ty Cobb, not Babe Ruth."

"Oh, how you used to make love to me. And when I became pregnant, we'd meet in Central Park and you'd tell me how beautiful I was and how you could never stop looking at me." She looks down at her plate sighing. "Then you graduated medical school and never looked at me again."

"But I never looked at anyone else."

"One night I went down to the river and the memories didn't seem to work anymore." Susan lapses into silence.

Feld waits, and finally speaks. "Okay, then what?"

"Oh, I remembered the woman who jumped, and then as I thought about our kids, this nice young man came up to me. It was then Bernie that I knew."

"Knew what?"

"That it was over between us. He sat on a park bench with me and held me while I cried. I saw him a few times after that and he made me feel young and beautiful again."

Feld examined his fingernails. "How long did this affair go on?" he asks softly.

"It's long over. The point I am trying to make is that you didn't even know I was missing."

"I missed you all summer." Feld looks in Susan's eyes. "It's okay, it's over," he says gently.

"Oh really? You didn't attend your own son's graduation. If I recall correctly, you were delivering a talk to doctoral candidates at Princeton. He told his friends who asked that 'My father's a very busy guy.' I complained, but it did no good, for when Beth finished medical school, so proud to follow your example, she had to tell her classmates that you could not come because you were engaged in important research. What was it? Something about family bonding of fish."

"Whales," he corrects. "Bonding of whales."

She shrugs. "Whatever. I only recall you found a very close-knit family structure. If one lay dying on the beach, the others would not abandon it and end up dying also."

"That's the difference between whales and humans. They're more loyal."

"But you're not dying, Bernie, just your family around you."

"You realize, don't you, my research and practice paid for all that quality education our kids received?"

Susan lets out an extended sigh. "You *still* don't get it, do you? Oh, as a professional, you hit one of those 'grand slam home runs' you always talk about. The kids and I? We're just your cheerleaders."

"Come on Susan, we're a winning team. I win, you win, the kids win, and we all win!"

"Winning? It's more than getting a table at a fine restaurant, or sending our children to Ivy League schools."

"Give me a break. Everything you have, and the kids have, is thanks to my work. I won it for you. But for my success, you'd likely be teaching in high school or running for coffee in some business office."

"See? You cannot even conceive that I could be running a business office."

She pushes her chair back and gets up. He reaches over and grabs her arm.

"Susan, don't leave–please. You must understand; everything I did was for you–and for the kids."

"Oh yeah? Bernie, what's your daughter's middle name?"

"Oh come on, Susan."

"Uh huh. And on what day is your son's birthday?"

He shakes his head and releases her arm.

"And our anniversary?"

Feld sits silently.

"It was the tenth of last month. That's why I invited you to the Cape. I thought . . . Oh, never mind.

"Admit it, Bernie. Am I right?"

Feld shrugs. "Well, you seem to know exactly who I am and how I feel."

"Wish I did Bernie, I really do, but the fact is that I don't know. Do you know who you are? How you feel? What about right now? What are you feeling? I'll bet you don't have a clue. You know why? Because you live your life through your patients. You spend your time solving their problems so you don't have to face your own."

"Don't denigrate my patients. They gave you and me a very good life."

"Bernie, for twenty-eight years, do you think we ever had real intimacy? Other than those first years, I don't think so. You've never been present for me, the children, or for that matter, yourself."

Susan holds out her hand to him and her eyes meet his. But he sits frozen in his chair. "See what I mean, Bernie. Look, I'll make very plain."

"Susan, please don't leave. Let's talk."

"There's nothing to talk about. I want this divorce, period. While you were arranging for a cemetery plot for your father in Israel, I spent my summer grieving and saying *my* goodbyes. My lawyer will call yours. Let's make this easy, okay?"

She turns on her heel and walks out of the restaurant at a brisk pace.

Feld watches her leave. He pours himself the remainder of the martini from the container.

Chapter 7

Feld leaves the Tavern On The Green, turns right, and strolls through Central Park along the path bordering Sheep Meadow, a vast expanse of open park stretching from Sixty-Sixth to Sixty-Ninth Streets on the west side of the park. He'd heard there really were sheep in that meadow until sometime in the 1930s when park czar, Robert Moses, supposedly banished them to Prospect Park in Brooklyn. Well, apparently Moses accomplished his purpose. New Yorkers of all ages were enjoying this meadow sans sheep, lolling on the grass or playing ball.

His stroll takes him past one of the many baseball diamonds in the park. He stands against the wire fence watching a pick-up game. He sighs. As tempting as it is to join in, he is neither dressed for it nor does he have the time. He never has the time. *Susan was right. I blew away my son's graduation so I could speak to doctorial graduates at Princeton. The great Dr. Feld receives another honor! For what? I did the same thing to my daughter, who had looked up to me as a shining example. How pathetic! I don't deserve a loving family.*

He watches a young man stroke the ball between the right and center fielders, ending up at second base with a double. *I was good enough to make the Columbia baseball team, I'm sure of it. Who knows? I could have been the next in line of Columbia ball players who made it to the major leagues. Now it's nothing but a daydream—there's no baseball for me and soon, there'll be no family either.*

"Hey you!" The shout ended his reverie. He looks up. The catcher points to home plate. "Wasn't that guy out at home? Didn't you see me put the tag on him?"

Feld shrugs. "Sorry fella, I was looking the other way." The catcher continues the argument with the opposing players. Feld moves on; time to return to his office. He heads to the other side of the park on one of the many east-west walkways.

His thoughts return to public blowup with Susan at the restaurant, but not for long. A baseball bounces up against his ankle, once again interrupting his musings. He bends down and picks up. He isn't near any of the baseball fields. He looks to see where it might have come from.

"Hey, mister, that's my ball!"

Feld turns and sees a nine or ten-year-old boy running toward him holding a baseball bat. Feld smiles and tosses the ball to the young boy.

A woman comes running after the boy, arriving breathless. She grabs the boy's arm. "I told you, stop disappearing on me."

She looks at Feld. Shock registers on her face. "Dr. Feld? What are *you* doing here on the West Side?"

He smiles. "Hello Dyan, I lunched at Tavern On The Green with my . . . uh, a colleague."

Regan affectionately pats the boy's head. "Dr. Feld, this is the love of my life, Bobby. Bobby, say hello to Dr. Feld."

"Hi, Dr. Feld." Bobby extends his hand.

Feld takes his hand. "Nice to meet you Bobby."

"Gosh, Dr. Feld, my mom says your office is full of baseball stuff. I'm a baseball player myself—in the Little Leagues."

"Really? What position do you play?"

"Oh, I pitch, but I'm a good hitter, too."

Feld smiles. "I'll bet you are."

Bobby nods. "What's your favorite team, Dr. Feld?"

Regan clucks. "Now, Bobby, stop asking so many questions. Give him a break."

Bobby shrugs. "Hey, we're going to have a picnic. Wanna' come?"

"I'd like nothing better, Bobby, but I have to be somewhere in a few minutes."

"Dr. Feld is a busy man, Bobby."

"Aw, come on, Dr. Feld. Then you can tell me all about your baseball stuff."

Regan puts her hands on her hips and glares at her son. "Bobby, that's enough!"

But the boy will not be deterred. "Hey, can we go to a baseball game some time?"

Feld laughs. "You really love baseball, don't you, Bobby?"

"Yeah. You must, too, because you have all that great baseball stuff in your office."

Regan pushes Bobby away. "Well, unlike you, Dr. Feld, Bobby and I haven't had our lunch yet. Been too busy chasing this rascal and his ball around the park." She squeezes Bobby's shoulder. "See that blanket and picnic basket over there in the grass?" She points. "We'll be over there if you should change your mind."

Regan pushes Bobby in front of her and heads him toward the blanket. But the boy pulls away and turns to Feld. "You can have some of my baseball cards if you come right now."

"I really can't. I'm you mother's doctor."

"But you're not her doctor right now."

"Bobby, leave Dr. Feld alone."

Bobby ignores her. "Don't you like baseball cards?"

Feld nods. "Sure, I have a large collection."

"Ever hear of Bobby Thompson, Dr. Feld?"

Feld smiles. "I'll never forget him. In the ninth inning he hit a three-run home run for the New York Giants against the Brooklyn Dodgers that won the pennant for his team."

"I have a card of him in his rookie season. See ya." Bobby turns and walks away.

"One moment young man," Feld calls out. "What condition?"

"Brand new, the gum's still wrapped with it. Wanna see it?"

Feld shuffles his feet and has a look of resignation. Regan shrugs and spreads her arms as if to say, "What can I do?"

Feld approaches them on the grass. "I haven't had an offer like that in a long time."

Bobby runs over and takes his hand. "Great, we're right over there. Let's go."

Bobby pulls Feld along to the blanket while Regan spreads out the drinks and food.

Regan looks at Feld and shrugs. "Sorry about all this."

"No, it's okay, really."

Bobby bites into the chicken leg. "Who's your favorite team? The Yankees?"

Regan shakes her head. "Don't talk with your mouth full, it's not polite."

Feld takes a sip of lemonade and looks up at the sky, studying the cloud formations as if they were a series of Rorschach tests. "My team left New York a while ago."

"The Giants! You rooted for the Giants?"

Feld smiles. "Not quite. I'll give you a hint. Ever hear of Jackie Robinson?"

"Sure did. He was the first Black player to play baseball."

"That's not quite correct, Bobby. There were many, many Black baseball players. It's just that they could never play in the major leagues."

"Because of discrimination, right?"

"Right. But the Brooklyn Dodgers broke the color barrier. Branch Rickey, its owner, said discrimination was no good and hired Robinson to play for them. The Dodgers were my team and I was very proud of them."

Bobby frowned and eyed Feld suspiciously. "And that's why you rooted for the Dodgers, because they let Robinson play on their team?"

"That was one important reason, but there were others too."

"Such as?"

"Well, I guess rooted for the underdog. The Dodgers didn't win very often. Some even called them the 'Brooklyn Bums'." Feld turned his head to look at Regan. "But they always tried very hard, putting their hearts into every game. I liked that and learned a very important lesson from them."

"What did you learn?" Bobby asked.

"Don't give up, that's what I learned. Whatever happens, don't give up."

"No, you just move to Los Angeles," Regan harrumphed.

Feld puts his face close to Bobby's. "Did you hear something, Bobby?"

"Nah, nothing. Do you like the Yankees?"

"Nope, the Yankees always win. Besides, it was always the Yankee fans that called the Dodgers 'the Bums'."

Regan smiles. "As he says, Dr. Feld likes the underdog."

"That's right. Struggling against the odds builds character, Dyan."

Tired of sitting on the blanket, Bobby stands up, looking down at Feld. "Any other reasons you liked the Dodgers?"

Feld smiles. "Yes, because I'm from Brooklyn."

"Aha, so that's your deep, dark secret," Regan says, a twinkle in her eyes.

Feld turns to Bobby. "Most of us mystery men come from Brooklyn. You know when I was young and handsome–just like you–I used to ride the old BMT subway train to Ebbets Field."

"You took the subway?"

"Yes, Bobby. But to me it was not merely a subway, but my magic carpet that took me to an enchanted place. I saved up money to go to the games–collected empty soda bottles and returned them to the grocery store for the deposit. I'd get two cents for the small ones and a whole nickel for the big bottles. Then I earned money by delivering groceries and when I had enough money, I'd take the train to my enchanted place, Ebbets Field, buy a ticket, and see a game.

"But sometimes I'd go to the ballpark and just hang around outside, waiting for the players to come out."

Bobby frowned. "Why didn't you go inside?"

"I didn't have the money for a ticket. Besides, my father didn't like baseball and he was saving all his money so I could become a doctor."

"What about your mom?"

"She wasn't living with us and my father said it was a waste of money."

Feld catches Regan staring at him.

Bobby shakes his head. "So you just hung out outside the park?"

Feld smiles. "Want to know why?"

Bobby nods. "Tell me."

"Because some of the players took the BMT from Ebbets Field back to the old St. George Hotel where they stayed when in town. I'd get on that train too, and talk to them. They were nice guys who would shoot the breeze with me. Guys like Gil Hodges, Duke Snider, Roy Campanella, Pee Wee Reese, Carl Furillo–they'd all talk to me."

"What about Jackie Robinson?"

"No, Bobby, he was gone by then."

"Wow, that must have been exciting."

Feld nodded. "For a young boy, it was very exciting. The players on the train even gave me a special name."

"They did? What did they call you?"

"Well, one day on the train Pee Wee Reese asked me what position I played. I had hoped that Pee Wee would invite me to join the Dodgers. Of course, all of this wishful thinking was just in the back of my mind."

"What did you tell him?"

"The truth. That I couldn't pitch very well but I was super at catching fly balls and was one heck of a good hitter."

"So did he ask you to try out for the team?"

"Nope. But he turned to Duke Snider and said, 'Hey, Duke, you better be careful; this kids sounds like one hell of an outfielder.' "

"No kidding? That must have been really neat."

"There's more. A week later, Duke Snider gave me his fielder's glove. He even wrote on the back of it."

"What?" Bobby said impatiently.

"To Bennie, the outfielder."

"Wow, neat!"

Regan, mesmerized, watched closely this interaction between her psychiatrist and her son.

"Well, Bobby, it wasn't quite that neat. You see, my name is not Bennie, it's Bernie. "

All three of them laughed.

Bobby is still wide-eyed about the glove. "You still have it?"

"Sure do. It's in my office. I'll be sure to show it to you sometime."

"That would be neat. Dr. Feld. Can we have a catch some-time?"

"We'll see." Feld looks at his watch and shakes his head. "It's getting late. I really have to get back to my office." He shakes Bobby's hand. "It was great meeting you Bobby. I had a real nice time."

Regan already begins to gather up the food and utensils, shaking out the blanket. "Bobby, I'm going to take this garbage over to the trash container. Dr. Feld, we had a good time. If you're not here when I get back, I'll see you at our next session—and thanks for regaling my son. Come, Bobby."

"Aw Mom, can't I stay here and say goodbye to Dr. Feld?"

She looks at her son for a few moments. "Well. . . all right, but don't you dare move away from this blanket."

Bobby grabs Feld's hand. "Come on, I'll pitch you a couple of fastballs–over by that big tree."

"Not today, Bobby. I'm not having your mother coming down hard on me."

Bobby ignores the admonition and hands Feld the bat.

Feld holds the bat, his hands on his hips. "We can't play ball here, someone may get hurt. That's what they have the ball diamonds for."

"No one will get hurt. Look around, there's no one here. Please? One pitch?" Bobby walks toward the big tree.

"Not today, Bobby. Let's get back to the blanket before your mother has a fit."

"Oh, come on. Afraid I'll take you down swinging."

Feld looks around the field. *Bobby's right, it is empty.* He removes his suit jacket and rolls up his sleeves. "Okay, one pitch–and I'm bunting."

"All right! Ready?"

Feld takes a batter's stance and Bobby throws a low fastball. He doesn't swing. "They must have lowered the strike zone since I last played."

Feld picks up the ball and tosses it back to Bobby.

"Aw, that's 'cause I'm used to pitching to kids. We have lower knees, you know."

Feld laughs.

Bobby looks around, as if there are men on base, takes a shortened windup and fires the ball just above Feld's waist. Feld swings and misses, losing his balance.

Bobby runs to him. "You all right? I'm sorry; I thought you were just going to bunt."

"Get back to the pitcher's mound," Feld growls.

"All right!"

Feld digs in, plating his feet firmly; his eyes concentrate on the ball in Bobby's hand. Once again, Bobby winds up and tosses a fastball. This time there's a loud piercing crack that could probably be heard throughout Sheep's Meadow. Bobby's head swivels and his mouth drops open as he follows the soaring baseball higher and higher. It lands some four hundred and fifty feet away.

"Holy shit, holy shit! Dr. Feld, that was some shot."

"Holy what, young man?" Bobby whirls around to see his mother descending upon him. "If I ever hear you use that word again, you'll be on the first train to Boys Town."

"Sorry, Mom. But did you see that shot Dr. Feld hit? Just like a rocket, better than Babe Ruth, Roger Maris, or Mickey Mantle. Never seen anything like it!"

Regan shakes her finger at Bobby. "Well, young man, you'll have plenty of time to remember that hit. You are grounded!"

"Aw Mom, that ain't fair."

"'Isn't' fair, not 'ain't' fair. You disappeared for the fourth time today and gave your mother another fright. That isn't fair either."

"Grounded? For how long?"

Regan looks up, rubbing her chin. "Well, let's just see. Four disappearances and a few 'holy shits'. Let's say you're down for a week." She whirls around to face Feld.

"You're grounded too, Dr. Feld." She extends her hand and grabs his, smiling. "Goodbye, Dr. Feld. You're not to leave your office until our next session."

Feld nods and starts to walk away. Regan catches up to him. She touches his hand. Their eyes meet.

"Thanks. You're a good man, doctor. "

She plants a lingering kiss on his cheek.

Chapter 8

There's a light rapping on his office door. Feld stops writing on his note pad. "Come in."

"Here's the plant I promised you." Dyan hands him a potted bloom.

"Thank you."

She smiles sheepishly. "You really don't have to take your father's picture down. Sorry about what I said at our last session."

"Don't worry about it. It needed a dusting anyway. How are you doing?"

She sits down. "Not good."

"What's the matter?"

She shrugs. "Frankly, I don't know what's going on any more."

"Explain."

She shakes her head. "Confused, very confused."

"I'm not surprised, you should be confused. After all, you are working through a lot of difficult issues."

"No, this is different. This is like nothing else I've ever faced."

"Look, Dyan, don't be discouraged. Things are moving along as they're supposed to. We're on schedule. Have you had any more asthma attacks?"

"No, I'm fine on that score. What kind of a 'schedule' am I on? For a nervous breakdown?"

"I doubt that very much."

"Look, before I came here six months ago, I had problems like anyone else, but I could manage them."

"Really? Let's put this in perspective. Six months ago, you were hooked on prescription drugs, you had already lost three jobs, had a history of involvement with an abusive man, and you were on the verge of losing custody of your son." Feld had ticked off each point on his fingers. "You seem to forget all that. Now, you've got a job and managed to avoid destructive relationships. And most important, you have a fighting chance to keep your son."

Regan runs her fingers through her hair. "Look, I'm sorry about kissing you the other day. I was just acting out."

"I know. But it's okay. I'm not sorry. I needed a kiss."

"You won't hurt me by reporting this to the courts, will you?"

"No, I won't hurt you, certainly not for a kiss. But one thing I must consider is your health and Bobby's welfare. Will you trust me?"

She sighs. "Well, I want to keep my son, that's for sure."

Feld shakes his head. "I want that too, but wanting to keep Bobby and trusting are two different things."

Regan nods. "Look, I'll try, I really will."

"Good, we've settled that. Now tell me, what's going on with you?"

"Next month is Bobby's tenth birthday. I'm planning a party for him. But you're all he talks about."

"It's understandable. We both love baseball."

"Yeah, but he wants you to come to his party. He loved your stories about the Dodgers. Told all his friends and asked them if they have any Dodger baseball cards. He talks about that day in the park non-stop."

"I'm flattered, I really am, but it would not be good for your treatment. For that matter, it would not be good for me as your therapist."

"What about the other day–in the park?"

"A very nice day. But Dyan, I'm your therapist and here to help you understand and deal with issues that interfere with a normal life. Taking this relationship outside the office would not only be unethical on my part, it would destroy the whole treatment process."

She folds her arms across her chest. "Bobby will be disappointed, very disappointed."

"I'm sure you can explain it to him so that he'll understand. Now, why don't you lie down on the couch? Make yourself comfortable."

She grins wickedly. "Care to join me?"

Feld gives her a tolerant smile. "In spirit only, Dyan."

She lies on the couch, but with her back to Feld.

"Ready to face some of your monsters, Dyan?"

"I'll leave them right where they are, thank you–in my dreams."

"That's not the way to get to the root of your problems and find out what's bothering you. How about hypnosis? Do you recall we discussed that possibility earlier?"

"I also recall telling you there's no way I can subject myself to that."

"Look, it's not just hypnosis. I can administer a sedative beforehand, which will relieve the stress and relax your inhibitions."

Dyan laughs harshly. "Then what, doctor? I start confessing to all those murders I have buried deep down inside of me?"

"That would be one possible outcome–if you've committed such murders. However, you'd still be safe because I'm not allowed to tell anyone. Just don't tell me about murders you are planning to commit. Those confidences aren't protected. You aren't planning any such crimes, are you?"

"Believe me; I've had my moments . . ."

Feld looks at her hard and steady. "Enough banter. Let's get down to the real world. Tell me, are you taking your asthma medicine since we last talked to me?"

"And if I haven't?"

"Dyan, you promised you would work with me."

"Okay already. I've been taking the damn stuff."

"Good."

Regan swings her feet off the couch and sits up, looking at Feld. "Look Doctor, I'll make a bargain with you. You come to my son's birthday party and I will let you hypnotize me. A deal?"

Fled shakes his head. "I just can't. But I will get Bobby a birthday present."

She sighs and lies back down on the couch. "Sorry, doctor, I really have no right to . . ."

Feld interrupts. "Yes, you do have a right to ask because I had a good time with you and Bobby in the park, and I told you that."

She nods.

"Now, before we go into hypnosis, tell me what you remember about the first time you had an asthma attack."

She shakes her head vigorously. "No! I simply don't want to remember that!"

"Approach it indirectly. It will be less frightening. Start with simple little facts. The kind of day it was, what you were wearing, how old you were. Stuff like that."

"I was five or close to it. It must have been fall because I could smell burning leaves. Well, maybe it was early winter because I was wearing my heavier red coat, mittens, and my shiny black Mary Jane shoes. I remember my feet were cold and I kept stamping them in the leaves to keep warm. I put a few of the leaves in my pocket to play with later." Dyan hugs herself tightly, looks up at the ceiling.

"Anything the matter?"

"Yeah. The leaves–they dirtied my shoes and I had dirt in my pocket where I put them. Mrs. Doyle slapped my hands and turned out my pockets. Made me throw the damn leaves away."

"This Mrs. Doyle–she was your foster mother?"

"One of many."

"So she threw the leaves away. How did you react?"

"I screamed that she wasn't my mother and couldn't tell me what to do." Then I promptly picked up the leaves and put the right back in my pocket."

"And her reaction?"

"She made me get rid of the leaves. I threw a tantrum, so she slapped me hard and said if I didn't stop that wailing, she'd trade me in for a good girl."

"Anything else you recall?"

"Yeah, Mrs. Doyle told me if I behave, she'd buy me a special present. So we went to different stores, just walking and walking until my feet were cold and hurt, and I was exhausted. I sat down on a stoop to rest. That made Mrs. Doyle very angry and she pulled me off the stoop and literally dragged me along." Regan rubs her brow and then runs her fingers through her hair. "Look, Doctor, I really don't feel comfortable with this; I don't want to go on."

Feld studies her closely. "I'm not surprised. I know this is scary for you. Dyan, I promise we'll stop whenever you wish, but I urge you to just try to go a little further."

Wary, she frowns. "How much further? To the edge?"

He gives a fractional shrug. "If you get to that point, I assure you, I won't let you fall over. Dyan, can you trust me for a little while longer?"

She nods, almost imperceptibly. "Doyle did buy some things. I recall a hat–a red, woolen one. Doyle held it up to show me; said it was a boy's hat."

Feld purses his lips. "A boy's hat? Was it for one of your foster brothers?"

"You guessed it. For the one who used to put his finger inside me. Anyway, we continued walking, she half dragging me when I stopped at one of the store windows. Mrs. Doyle would have none of that and tried to pull me away, but I dug my heels in and wouldn't move."

43

Feld waits for her to continue, but she just lies there. He sighs. *"Okay,* now what was in the window?"

"A violin."

"A violin? What did you know about violins that you wanted one?"

Regan gets up, strolls over to the window and looks out. "The summer before," she says, still looking out the window, not at Feld, "I was all dressed up in my pretty white dress. I even had a big flower pinned to it. I came across an old man playing a violin while he sat under a big tree. People were putting money into his hat that he'd put out by his feet. He played beautiful music. It made me feel sad and happy at the same time. I skipped over to Mrs. Doyle and asked her for some money to put in the violinist's hat. He was so alone and I felt really sorry for him." Regan leaves the window and flops back on the couch. She bends forward and puts her head in both hands.

"Let the feelings come to the surface, Dyan."

She bites her lip. "It's there, I know it's there, but I just can't find it."

"Okay. Tell me, how did you feel when you asked Mrs. Doyle for the money? I assume she refused to give it to you."

"I guess I felt damn angry. She not only refused to give me any money, she just wouldn't pay any attention to me because she was flirting with the man sitting next to her on the park bench. I kept asking her until she finally told me to shut up and behave. So I tried to tear off the flower pinned to my dress. I could only get it half off so that it just dangled there at an odd angle. She made me wear just like that for the rest of the day and I didn't feel pretty anymore."

Regan stands up and glares at Feld, her eyes blazing. "Look, damn it, this is just getting too much for me."

"Just relax, Dyan, you're doing fine. Take your time."

Regan nods and sits down. "I told Doyle that she wasn't my real mother and couldn't boss me around. Doyle turns to her man friend and told him, 'Her real mother was likely some little tramp.'" Regan laughs.

"What's so funny?"

"After she called my mother a tramp, I immediately pictured Charlie Chaplin, and for a long time, I told people my real mother. . ." Dyan laughs again, ". . . was Charlie Chaplin."

Feld rubs his chin, holding Regan in a steady gaze. "Anything else you can recall?"

Regan pauses pensively, rubbing her forehead with her fingers. "Well, let's see. I recall walking away from them and returning to the man playing the violin. At first he was lost in his playing, you know how a violinist can be. Then he finally noticed me. He stood up, put the violin in one of my arms, and rested it on my shoulder. He handed me the bow and said, 'You try.' I ran the bow across the strings. The sound was unbelievably horrible. When I finished, the old man immediately began applauding and, reaching down into his hat, pulled out a dime, and handed it to me. I threw myself into his arms."

Regan begins laughing again.

"Now what's so funny?"

"Oh, I was just thinking how red the old man turned. The poor guy didn't know what to do. He saw how I was hurting. I said I had no money to give him. He just smiled and pointed to the bedraggled flower half off my dress. Then asked me if he could have it. He helped me remove it from my dress and then I gave it to him."

Regan stops talking and examines her hands.

"Why don't you continue?"

Regan nods. "Well, he began to play that violin just for me. I'll never forget the melody, I can recognize anywhere. I did not know the name of the piece until much later. It was *Humoresque.* After awhile, Mrs. Doyle called to me and we left the park. Then she noticed I wasn't wearing the flower. I wouldn't tell her what I did with it and soon I ended up in my third foster home. Undoubtedly I must have been quite a little terror."

"No, you were simply a lonely little girl."

Regan shakes her head and laughs harshly. "Why don't you tell me something I don't already know?" She stands and straightens her skirt. "That's enough for now. Thanks for your time but I don't think I can handle any more today."

"I know dredging up these memories can be very upsetting. That's just part of the process and these memories have to surface. That's also why you feel like running away now."

"You're not listening to me. I can't handle this anymore. At least not for today." She heads for the office door, placing her hand on the doorknob.

"Dyan, please, sit down. You really can handle more. You're a lot stronger than you give yourself credit for." Feld spreads his arms. "But it's your choice."

"Ha! You don't think I'll come back, do you?"

"It's possible. You're at the stage where you very well might run away."

"You want me to come back?"

"Of course I do."

"Then I'll see you next week." She opens the door. "I'll be back. Frankly, I don't give a damn what you think. I know I'm not a frightened child who runs away from everything."

"I'll be here. But whatever is frightening you will follow you out that door."

"Trying to scare me? You can do better than that. Try something like 'if you go out the door, you'll go off a bridge, or run in front of a bus.' "

Feld studies her silently.

She explodes. "Jesus, what do you want from me?"

"For you to get better. I simply want you to get better." He gets up and walks over the Regan. "Look, you're emotions are close to the surface. You are able for the first time to access childhood memories. You're close to a breakthrough."

Regan flashes a sardonic smile. "You mean a 'breakdown', don't you?"

"Therapy is not like reading a book where you can always go back to the precise point you left off reading. If you leave now, your resistance could come back in full force and it could take months to reach point again. I suggest we try hypnosis–now."

"No way, not now."

"Then I'll see you next week." She slams the door behind her.

Feld shakes his head.

The intercom buzzes. "Dr. Edelstein is waiting to see you."

Feld leans back in his chair. "Send him right in, Arlene."

Chapter 9

Feld gets up and holds out his hand. "Great to see you Saul."

Dr. Saul Edelman, 68, a distinguished doctor heading Columbia Medical Center in New York City, and formerly Feld's analyst, shakes Feld's hand warmly. "Come on in. Can I offer you a drink? Some lunch?"

Edelman shakes his head. "Just the drink–a scotch and soda. I never have lunch in the afternoon."

Feld hands him his drink and pours a plain club soda for himself. Feld looks at Edelman and shrugs. "I'm working."

"Ah, club soda. Dr. Feld, always the sober man on the job. I'm not seeking therapy, so I hope you're not going to charge me for this visit. Rumor has it that you are very expensive."

Feld laughed. "No, I called to see you, remember?"

"So what's so important to pull me away from my very busy schedule?"

"Sorry about that."

Edelman smiles. "No need for apologies, I was just being facetious. So what's up?"

Feld looks down at his hands. "It's the anniversary of my father's death."

"Bernie, look at me."

Feld lifts his head and their eyes meet.

"You will need a lot more than club soda to talk about your father."

Feld sighs. "It's not that at all. It's just that I get a little down at this time of the year. Magnify things out of proportion, I guess."

"Are you worried about the offer of the board of directors of Columbia General to run our little mental health empire when I retire in three months?"

Feld purses his lips. "Honored, yes, but not worried. You can inform the board that I gratefully accept." He raises his glass in the gesture of a toast, clinking with Edelman's glass. "I have finally arrived, reaching the top of the hill."

Edelman guffawed. "More like the top of the heap! You can't believe the bullshit and politics that goes on there–more like a third-world country. And I hate to tell you this, but the Psychiatric Department is the worst of the worst, what with trying to keep their state and federal funding, and constantly seeking out more grants and endowments."

"Why me?"

"To be brutally honest, the board of trustees is not in the business of making your dreams come true. Frankly, the board chose you because of your ambition, which the board feels can be put to good use on its behalf. And when the Hasidim found out your father was a doctor who survived Auschwitz, it was a *mechaieh*, a real joy, for them."

"You don't have to translate. I understand Yiddish."

"Sorry. In any event, they threw their full support behind your appointment. Also, don't forget that seventy-five percent of the doctors at Columbia General are ardent supporters of Israel. It doesn't hurt that the Israeli government will dedicate a cemetery to your father's memory–for them it's kind of like Moses parting the Red Sea. Besides, you are a distinguished alumnus of P&S."

"I'm honored to accept, especially for such an *unbiased* appointment."

Edelman lets the comment pass. He stands up and raises his drink. "To your appointment." They clink their glasses again.

Edelman sits down. "The board meets three weeks from Thursday. I'll let you know when it's official. No need for you to worry, the vote is more or less just a 'rubber stamp'."

Feld nods silently.

Feld stares out the window for a few seconds and sighs. "You know, on his death bed, I promised my father that he'd be buried in Israel, his final resting place. But right now I have some other personal matters that preoccupy me."

Edelman smiles. "Don't tell you're having an affair with my wife."

"Fraid not, though she's been after me to run away with her. Out of loyalty to you, I declined the invitation."

Edelman snickers. "Some friend you are."

Feld rubs his chin. "Seriously, Saul, I've been treating a patient for a year and a half and I feel I'm close to a major breakthrough with her."

"And?"

"And–I'm experiencing, or rather I should say, I am concerned that my feelings have evolved into more that a doctor/patient relationship."

Edelman shrugged. "So? In your case, I'd really be concerned if the patient was a male. You want to fuck her. I understand that, because it's normal. Me? I want to fuck my secretary. As a matter of fact, I want to fuck your secretary as well."

Feld frowned. "Very funny. You planning to do some comedy in the Catskills?"

Edelman laughs out loud. "Touché. Sorry about that; my mind is already on retirement–and sex. But as far as the sex part is concerned, it's all just in my mind."

Edelman rubs his chin. "Tell me, Bernie, is this patient solicitous?"

"Not really, but I think she has feelings for me. It's not just sexual, transference or counter-transference, or some other clinical bullshit.

I really have feelings for her. That's the problem. This is very difficult . . . . I dream of her and sometimes I wake up sobbing, other times I wake up with a joyous feeling I've never had before."

Edelman rolls his eyes. "Come on, Bernie, I don't have to explain this to you. You're one of the best psychiatrists in the business!"

Feld sits silent, tugging at his ear. His eyes meet Edelman's. "She has a son who loves baseball. I spent an hour in the park with them. It brought back a lot of my old memories–some of them very painful."

"An hour in the park? That's it? Bernie, you are really pushing the envelope."

"Actually, it was quite harmless. I had just come off a meaningful lunch with Susan when I bumped into them in the park."

"Meaningful lunch with Susan? What's that mean?"

"Let's fight one dragon at a time, Saul."

"Okay, then let's back up. It's the anniversary of your father's death. Does that suggest anything to you?"

"I guess. Her kid, baseball, my childhood. Seems to be all mixed together. Everything is very complicated and confused."

"Are you feeling guilt because you might have enjoyed yourself in the park? Do you feel you're falling in love with this patient of yours?"

Feld shrugs. "I don't know what to think."

"Bernie, I asked what you 'feel', not what you think."

"It's not clear what I feel."

"Don't over analyze it. I hear you say you feel out of control and don't like it. Just remember, Bernie, your wife's been at the Cape all summer. You and she probably have some problems to work out; your kids are building their own lives right now. So feeling lonely and powerless is both appropriate and normal. It's situational; I'm sure of it, so don't pick at it and it will go away."

"That's easy to say Saul, but I've been in practice for over twenty years and I tell you it concerns me that I am going over the line."

"What line?"

"The doctor-patient line."

"You sure that's your worry? Frankly, to me it sounds like you're afraid of going not over a line, but a very high wall. Look, if you like we can work on that in therapy."

"Jeez, Saul I don't need a mentor anymore. As a matter of fact . . ."

Edelman finishes Feld's sentence, ". . . you don't need anyone."

Feld shakes his head. "No, I don't need a pop psychology session."

"Bern, I know I don't have to tell this, but if you get romantically involved with a patient, you'd lose the opportunity to chair the hospital, not to mention that it would ruin your marriage, your career, and be destructive to your patient."

Feld nods. "With Susan, it's gone much further than working out our problems. She wants a divorce and that's her final word."

Edelman sighs. "It seems when it rains, it pours. Sorry, that sounds a little callous and I didn't mean it that way. But I am confident you can handle all this, even the divorce."

"First my mother, then my father, and now Susan." He shakes his head slowly.

"Bernie, you can't assume all the blame and guilt. Your mother abandoned you when you were a young boy. Remember, in our therapy sessions, you never wanted to talk about it? Didn't you ever stop to wonder why she left?"

Feld shrugs. "I adjusted to her disappearance a long time ago."

"Are you absolutely sure, Bernie? As you know, I worked with many Vietnam veterans. Some had seen horrible things; others had committed them. But whether they were haunted by those they had killed or seen killed, they observed the same thing. The dying, whether American or the enemy, never called out for their wives or sweethearts. Their final cries were for their mothers. An important part of you died when your mother left—you need to cry out for her."

"I've already told you numerous times Saul; I have come to terms with that a long time ago. My father was the only one that mattered to me."

"But you never talk about him. My sense is that you saw him as a god-like figure, and what he said you accepted as the Gospel; that you gave up your dreams and whatever was left of your life to fulfill his."

"Why are you surprised? My father suffered unbelievable agony through four years in a concentration camp, or more accurately, a 'death camp'. You know how he survived? By reducing the suffering of others. He saved lives. He devoted his life and every penny he had to assure that I'd never have to suffer as he did."

Edelman frowns. "When I was in private practice, I always felt that you were one patient that I failed with. Do you know that? I could never get to deal with the issues regarding your father and his influence on you."

"But Saul, my father loved me and sacrificed his own medical career in this country by putting every penny he had towards my career. If it wasn't for my father, you'd be offering that hospital post to someone else."

"Face it, Bernie, your father sent you down the road to a career which, at best, only part of you wanted."

"Yeah, a road that led me to being one of the best physicians in New York."

"There are so many fields of medicine you could have pursued. Why psychiatry? Why not cardiology, surgery, or any other medical specialty?"

Feld leans back in his chair, eying Edelman. "I get it. You think I'm a 'wounded healer'."

"Bernie, you know that down deep we make choices that we really want to make. But we should also know *why* we made those choices. Consider coming back to analysis, I think you need it. There are things we can explore."

"Face it, Saul, you're retiring."

"Can you come for three months?"

"Ah, Saul, is that your ego talking? Want to redeem that 'sense of failure' in your practice?"

Edelman smiles slightly. "I'm too old to have an ego."

"You tapped me to run the hospital because I'm the best there is. Isn't that so, Saul? And how did I arrive at that plateau? My father instilled in me that there was only the 'best', there's no second place."

"You know very well, Bernie, that your father gave you no choice but to become a doctor. And you had to be the best. As a result, you didn't follow your dreams. If you had, you might have played center field for the New York Yankees and had your plaque up on the wall at Cooperstown. You are the outfielder that never was."

Bernie gets up, puts down his glass, strolls to the window, and stares out. "Saul, thanks for your advice on my patient." He turns away from the window and looks directly at Edelman. "We're not much different, are we Saul? You elbowed every competitor out of the way to get to the top; I had to break my ass to get it."

"That's a little cynical, isn't it? The fact is that I had a choice and I'm exactly who and where I want to be. No more, no less."

"Saul, I appreciate your recommendation for the position at the hospital."

Edelman nodded. "I'll tell the board of your acceptance. You'll do a great job. That much I am sure of. I won't say anything about your pending divorce until after the appointment. Meantime, let's get together for lunch before you take over at Columbia General."

Feld shakes hands with his visitor. "Enjoy your retirement–and thanks again."

Edelman heads for the door. He turns around. "Bernie?" Edelman shrugs. "Well, never mind." He closes the door behind him.

Feld sits and leans back in his desk chair, his arms folded in his lap, staring at the ceiling, thinking of Saul's comment, *the outfielder that never was.*

Chapter 10

Arlene sticks her head in the office. "Your three o'clock appointment, Dyan Regan, is here."

"Send her in."

"How are you, Dyan?"

"Okay, I guess. I want to thank you again for nice day in the park. Both Bobby and I enjoyed it."

Feld held her in a steady gaze. "I shouldn't have done that, you know. I want to apologize."

"Damn it, Dr. Feld, no apologies are necessary."

"Don't feel hurt. Understand, Dyan, I want you to get better. You're very close to a breakthrough and I don't want anything to interfere with that."

Regan sits down facing Feld. "Breakthrough? You mean a breakdown. You know what? You're a real son of a bitch, putting me through all that emotional turmoil and saying if I don't cooperate with you, I'll lose my son. We spent some good time together in the park and Bobby can't talk about anything else. Now you tell me it was a mistake and you apologize! What the hell do you want from me?"

"For you to work through your demons."

"Don't try to manipulate me. I've been manipulated by the best and compared to them you're a rank amateur."

"The last thing I want to do, Dyan, is to manipulate you. Remember we spoke about putting you under through hypnosis?"

She nods. "Yeah, and I also remember telling you that I doubt if it's something I can do–to let myself go under."

"Perhaps when you said that you weren't able to do so. But how do you feel *now?*"

"The same. I just don't want to explore what you call my 'inner depths' without my awareness."

"Well, I think now is the time to go ahead, while your feelings are close to the surface and your conscious mind is giving us information." He shrugs. "But if you're not ready, that's okay too. We can talk about it later."

Dyan leans forward. "Will it help me obtain a good report for the courts?"

"Yes, in the sense that it could very well speed up your recovery."

"Within the time for the legal deadline?"

"I certainly would hope so, but you must understand, there are no guarantees."

"And what if I can't go under? Will you hold that against me?"

"No, of course not."

Feld gets up and goes over a cabinet, unlocks it, and takes out a small bottle. He hands it to her. "Here, drink this sedative, it will relax you. We have plenty of time because I've rescheduled two other patients."

She looks into his eyes. "Manipulating me again, eh?" Not waiting for his answer, she downs the sedative in one gulp.

"Are you okay, Dyan?"

She has a broad smile and faraway look. "Oh just fit as a fiddle, Doc, fit as fucking fiddle. Like I'm getting a little high." She motions seductively with her head. "Come on over here and join me on the couch." Dyan pats the seat next to her.

He waits a minute and then begins to move his finger slowly

in front of her eyes, like a metronome. "Keep watching my finger and concentrate on my voice. We will count off the numbers from one to fifteen. I will say the odd numbers and you give me the even numbers. Do you understand?"

She nods.

By the eleventh number, Dyan is no longer counting.

He waits. She sits there, seemingly oblivious.

"Remove all feeling in your right arm. Now do you have any feeling in that arm?"

"No."

"Now close your eyes and extend your right arm."

Regan extends her arm, as instructed.

Feld leans over and jabs her lightly with a pin. "Do you feel any pain?"

"No."

"Anything at all?"

"No."

"Good. You can lower your arm, but continue to keep your eyes closed."

Regan drops her arm obediently.

"Excellent. Now I want you to go back in time to when you were five and a half. Can you do that?"

Regan nods.

"Good. Go back to that autumn day when you were walking with Mrs. Doyle and you passed that store window. Tell me what you see."

"I see a violin in the store window, just like the one the man in the park played." Her voice is that of an excited young girl.

"What happened after that?"

"Mrs. Doyle promised me," she says, a whine creeps into her voice.

"What did she promise?"

"A special present if I was good. I said I wanted that violin in the window, but Mrs. Doyle said no, that it cost too much and it wasn't a toy. She started to pull me away from the store window." Now Regan cries with little-girl tears. She squirms in the chair.

"Talk to Mrs. Doyle, Dyan."

"You promised." She stamps her foot on the carpeted office floor. "And I was good and I really want that violin. Please, Mrs. Doyle, I'll do anything." Regan cries in her five-year-old voice; the tears flow. "You don't ever have to get me anything else ever again. Please, Mrs. Doyle."

"And what did Mrs. Doyle say?"

Regan assumes a very angry adult tone, putting her hands on her hips. "You're just a brat, do you know that? You snivel and whine all the time and fight with my sons. You've been nothing but trouble since I've brought you home and you always want, want, want. The state doesn't pay me enough to put up with the likes of you. Now come along without another word or I promise you, you'll be on the first bus back to the home for kids."

Regan reverts to her little girl's pleading voice. "Please, I want this," pointing to the violin in the phantom store window. "Just like the man in the park had."

"What happened then, Dyan?"

Again assuming an adult voice, this time in an accusatory tone. "What man in the park? And just what were you doing with that man in the park?"

Regan brings her knees up to her chest, her head tucked behind her legs.

"Dyan, what's happening now? Why are you so upset?"

Regan begins bawling, her frightened voice barely understandable. "There's a policeman there. He's watching us. Mrs. Doyle tells me if I don't behave she'll turn me over to him."

"Dyan come back to the present, you are no longer five and a half."

Regan straightens up in her chair.

Feld studies her closely. "How old are you?"

"Thirty-nine."

"And where are you now?"

"In your office." Her tone turns sad and a little desperate. "I love you but you don't love me."

He pauses, leaning back in his chair.

"Dyan, do you recall when you had your asthma attack in the subway?"

"Yes."

"When, precisely?"

"When I saw the policeman."

"Did you see him before, during, or after the attack?"

"Just before I had the attack."

"Okay, Dyan. Now go back to being five and a half again. Return to when you were with Mrs. Doyle at the store window with the violin. Remember anything about that policeman?"

Once again, she speaks in the little girl's voice. "He was a very big man and Mrs. Doyle called him over. 'Officer, officer,' she said, 'come here and take care of this naughty little girl.' "

Regan takes several large gulps of air, her breathing becomes labored.

"What happening now, Dyan?"

"The policeman—he's walking toward me! I'm very frightened. My head is spinning round and round. Now it all goes black. Oh, God, I can't breathe." Regan hyperventilates as her attack grows worse. "Help me, help me, please! I can't breathe. I'm going to die, going to die like Mommy!"

Feld quickly moves to her side, grasping her by the shoulders. "Listen to me Dyan; you are not going to die! I won't let you. Do you understand? I promise, you won't die. Now go back before your first asthma attack. Can you do that? Go back before Mrs. Doyle, before the policeman. Go back to the last time you were with your real mother."

Regan continues to hyperventilate and then screams. Just as suddenly, she turns deathly silent for a few moments. Feld can see her transforming into an even younger child. Her voice and mannerisms follow suit.

"Please mommy, answer me. Please, I am scared." She shakes the cushion on the chair.

"Where are you now, Dyan?"

"At home," she replies, whimpering.

"And how old are you?"

"Three and a half." She curls up in chair. "I'm afraid," she moans. "The room is very dark and I can hear music playing. Mommy locked the doors and windows. She locked them all. Why did she put towels around the cracks in the doors? She's kneeling and praying to Baby Jesus. Mommy, what are you doing? Why are you praying to Baby Jesus?" Regan is crying.

"Dyan, why is she praying?"

Regan grabs her head in frustration. "I don't know, I don't know. She won't answer me. She is going into the kitchen and getting a bottle–I think it's whiskey."

"What's she doing now, Dyan?"

"Now she's pouring it into a very big glass. She's taking some medicine–lots of pills." Regan is crying and pleading, "Mommy, why are you crying? Please, Mommy, I'll be a good girl and clean my room. And tomorrow I'll clean it a million times better, I promise."

"What's happening now?"

Regan shakes her head and the tears flow freely. "She still won't answer me! All she does is go to bedroom and lie on the bed, still crying. She lifts me up; she puts her arms around me and kisses me. I can taste her tears. Then she shoves some of the medicine in my mouth." Regan grimaces. "Ugh, it tastes awful. I spit the stuff out." Regan reaches out, "Please Mommy, don't cry. I'll be good, starting right now. You'll see, I'll be the best little girl in the world."

Regan pushes away with both arms and begins grunting.

"Dyan, what's happening?"

"Mommy's falling asleep. She's lying on me and she's very heavy."

Regan struggles. "Don't go to sleep, Mommy, you're scaring me."

Regan starts singing to her mother. "She's not listening. Mommy! Mommy! Now Mommy raises herself up. Mommy wants to tell me something." Regan stops talking but continues to struggle.

"What is she trying to tell you? What does she say to you? It's important to remember."

"Sorry–she keeps saying she's sorry and crying. Mommy tries to get up but can't."

Regan flails her arms and jerks herself around violently.

"What's the matter? What are you doing now?"

Regan sobs. "Mommy has her hand and over my mouth and nose. I can't breathe! Mommy tells me not to breathe. I can't do that Mommy! Now she wants me to do something."

"What? What does she want you to do?"

"I don't know!" she cries out in a loud voice. Regan struggles again. "I can't move. I try but she is too heavy, and she's still holding me." Regan's struggles become more frantic. "I can't breathe."

The struggle stops.

"What's happening, Dyan?"

"Mommy lets go of my mouth. Don't go to sleep, Mommy. Please don't. I'm afraid and it's too dark in here.

"Now she wants me to do something."

"What does she want you to do?"

Now in a plaintive voice, "Something, but I'm too sleepy. What do you want me to do, Mommy? Mommy?"

"Dyan, please try to remember, it's very important."

"She wants me to turn off the music."

"What music? Dyan, tell me about the music."

"The record player is on and it's playing the song over and over."

"Do you recognize the song?"

Regan nods. "It's the same one that the old man played in the park."

Dyan rings her hands. Suddenly, she explodes out of the chair and searches all around the office. Feld hears her whimpering.

"No! No! It isn't the music; not the music she wants me to turn off."

""What does she want you to do? Think back. Remember."

"Turn it off; she wants me to turn off the music."

"No, Dyan, it's not the music. Remember, Dyan. What is it she wants you to turn off? If you remember, you can keep Bobby."

"The oven," she screams. "She wants me to turn off the oven and open the windows."

Regan, wild-eyed, leaps at Feld and begins shaking him.

"Mommy, please move; please get up. You're too heavy and I can't move. Please, Mommy, you're too heavy. Don't go to sleep, please. I'm very scared–very scared."

Regan breaks away from Feld and flops in the chair.

"What's happening, Dyan?"

"I'm getting out of the bed; it's hard. Now I'm out and crawling on the floor to the oven. I'm so close, but I fall asleep, right on the floor."

"When you wake up, what did you remember about what was happening?"

Regan is close to hysterical. "The monsters! The monsters wake me up. The room is filled with them–big heads and faces like elephants. Oh my God! They have axes and they are breaking everything–the doors, the windows. Now they are grabbing hold of mommy and hitting her. Leave my mommy alone! Now they are grabbing me and taking me to a window. They break the glass and try to push me out the window. I kick and hit them.

"No, please don't! I'll be good! I promise, I'll be good!"

"It's okay, Dyan. You're safe."

Regan stops crying and falls into a dead silence.

"Turn around, Dyan, and look at those monsters. Look at them and tell me what you see."

She shakes her head violently. "No, no, I won't look; I can't look, it's too dark." Still, she squints through the darkness.

"Dyan, listen carefully to me. If you don't look at those monsters, you'll lose Bobby."

Regan, in an adult voice, cries, "No, not Bobby. I want to keep him; he's a good boy."

"Then look at those monsters, Dyan, and tell me what you see."

"It's too dark."

She burrows into a corner of the chair. "Fire," she screams, again in a child's voice. "Fire everywhere! The whole room is burning up."

"Fire, Dyan? Is the room on fire?"

She burrows deeper. "Yes, fire! No, there are lights, lights flashing everywhere!"

Regan straightens up in the chair, then stands and walks around the office, trance-like. "Mommy, can you get up now. Please Mommy, move. Stop playing make-believe. You're really playing make-believe. Aren't you, Mommy?"

"What do the monsters look like, Dyan?'

"The monsters–they're only firemen and policemen." She wails. "Leave my mommy alone, leave her alone!" Regan flops down and cowers in a corner of the office.

"The policeman is shining a light in my eyes. He's yelling." Her voice becomes throatier. " 'I've got the kid. She's alive. She must have been playing with the gas in the oven.' Another policeman says, 'Tell her she just killed her mother.' "

"Dyan, it's not true, you did *not* kill your mother."

"No, Mommy wanted to turn off the gas and I didn't do it. I fell asleep instead."

"No, Dyan, your mother killed herself because she was very unhappy. It was she who turned on the oven. She, not you, turned on the gas. Do you understand that? She caused you to go to sleep by her actions. You did nothing bad."

Regan stands up and returns to the chair, her head down. "My mommy's dead, and I killed her," she said with resignation.

"You did not kill her," he corrects. "Dyan, it was your mother that took the pills. It was your mother that turned on the gas. Yes, your mommy is dead, but you did not kill her. When she asked you to turn off the gas, she tried to change her mind. But it was too late and she caused your sleepiness. Do you understand?"

She stares at him in bewilderment. "I think so," she mutters weakly.

"That's not good enough, Dyan. *Thinking so* won't do. I want you to know in your mind, and in your heart, and in your soul, that you did *not* kill your mother. Your mother was very, very sick and killed herself. Do you understand? You feel guilty because you survived and she did not, so you tortured yourself with your nightmares."

Regan sits up straight. "Mommy killed herself. She really did not want to but she killed herself anyway."

Feld leans forward, looking into her eyes. "That's right. She changed her mind at the last minute, but it was too late, and if the firemen and policemen didn't come in time, you'd be dead also. They saved you. Sometimes when the memory is very close to the surface and you see a policeman, it triggers an attack. Your mind created the asthma. Can you understand that?"

"Yes," she says softly.

"Good. When I end the hypnosis, you will remember what happened. The memory will be painful, but you will be strong enough to handle it. Can you do that?"

"Yes."

"You will find that in time, the memory will become less and less painful. Eventually, the memory will become a feeling of grief, not pain. Then the grief will turn to sadness and someday, the sadness will become acceptance. Do you understand?"

She nods. "Yes."

"Good. Now you know that what you thought were monsters were really policemen and firemen coming to save you. Your asthma was triggered whenever you saw a policeman because that was safer than confronting the memory of your mother's death and your belief, however false, that you killed her. Do you understand this?"

She nods. "But I want my mommy. Please bring my mommy back."

Dr. Feld puts his hand gently on her shoulder. "Let it out, Dyan Let those tears out."

After sobs become louder and louder she finally stops from exhaustion. She leans back on the couch, silent.

"Okay. Now, Dyan, I'm going to start to count. When I get to five, you will be out of your trance and back here with me. You will remember everything and be okay with it. One, two, three, four, *five.* Where are you now, Dyan?"

In her normal adult voice, "I am in your office with you."

"And who am I?"

Regan gets up with great effort, steps toward Feld, and on reaching him, collapses in his arms. He catches her and helps her back to the couch. He lays her down and gently covers her with his with his jacket. He bends down to kiss her, but thinks the better of it and straightens up.

Chapter 11

Feld looks at the building numbers on a street in lower Manhattan, checking with the number he had written on a slip of paper. Finally, the numbers match. He enters the building, steps in the elevator, and presses the button for the third floor. He hesitates, not sure this is a wise thing to do. *What the hell, I can't disappoint the kid on his birthday.* He finds the apartment number. It is not that difficult. He could hear the noise of the youngsters through the closed door. He rings the bell and puts a smile on his face.

The door opens. Dyan Regan greets him with an amazed look on her face. "Dr. Feld. This is a surprise! Come in, come in," grasping his arm and pulling him into the apartment.

"I was in the vicinity and thought I'd drop these presents off for Bobby." He offers her a full shopping bag.

"How sweet! But you should give it to Bobby yourself. He's in the other room. Come on, I'll take you to him. He'll be just delighted."

Feld doesn't move. "Before we do that, I wanted to let you know that I've filed a report with the court recommending that you retain custody for Bobby for the next six months. At the end of that period, if everything goes okay, I see no reason why you should not get a final decree in your favor and, of course, permanent custody."

Regan rises on her tiptoes and tenderly kisses Feld's cheek. "Thanks," she whispered in a voice cracking with emotion.

Feld shakes his head. "No thanks are necessary; you did on your own. You're a fine mother and I'm sure the judge will recognize that."

She nods. "I did the best I could. Unfortunately, bringing up a child does not come with an instruction manual."

As they enter the living room full of children playing games, Bobby spots Feld. He breaks off from a group and runs to the doctor. "Gosh, Dr. Feld, you came to my party!"

Feld smiles. "Here, Bobby, I brought these presents for you." Feld hands the boy the shopping bag.

Bobby dives into the bag and pulls out a baseball glove, handing it to his mother. "Look, Mom, Duke Snider's fielder's glove. Gee, Dr. Feld, thanks so much."

Regan examines the glove, crinkling her nose. "A little raunchy, isn't it? Well, at least it's not the player's socks."

"Gee whiz, Mom. What do you expect? Snider used that glove."

Feld laughed. "Pay no attention to her; she's just jealous she didn't get one."

Regan put Feld's hand in hers. "It was nice of you to come to the party."

"Wow, look, a real Yankee baseball cap." Bobby delves deeper into the bag. "And cleats! I've never had a pair of baseball cleats." Bobby kicks off his shoes and struggles to put on the cleats.

"They're perfect, Dr. Feld. They fit just right."

"Good, because I had to guess your size, figuring you could always return them for a proper fit."

"That was very thoughtful of you, Dr. Feld." She turns to her son. "Bobby, you owe him."

"So do you, Mom."

"Look, I'm off duty, so why don't both of you call me Bernie."

Music wafts through the room. Regan holds out her hand. "Why don't we go into the other room and celebrate Bobby's birthday with a dance?"

Feld does not move.

Bobby taps Feld on the leg. "Its' okay, Mom said she thought you were smart and handsome."

Regan blushes. "Bobby, stop telling tales out of school. All I said was my usual picture of a psychiatrist was with a pipe and beard."

Feld laughed. "That's how I looked in college. Okay Dyan, I accept your invitation, let's dance."

They walk into the other, less crowded room. Regan grabs both of Feld's hands and pulls him close to her. He could feel the outline of her body against his. He tightens up.

"You okay Dr. Feld?"

"Why do you ask?"

"The way you stiffened up."

Feld backs away. "Sorry."

Regan laughed. "No silly, I didn't mean it in a sexual way. Just that you went into, like, rigor mortis."

Feld pushes away from Regan. "I'm sorry, but I really must go."

"Oh come on, Dr. Feld–I mean Bernie–I was only kidding. Damn, for a psychiatrist you're really uptight."

"Sorry, Dyan, but we really shouldn't be doing this."

"That's the girl's line, not yours."

"Look, I'm in the middle of a divorce. Besides, I've never cheated on my wife and been with another woman."

Regan frowns. "Obviously, I don't run in your circles. Is that it?"

"Bobby," Regan shouts. "Come in here and say goodbye to Dr. Feld."

Bobby runs in. "But you just came. Can we see a Yankee game together sometime?"

Regan frowned. "Don't you remember? Dr. Feld is a rabid Dodger fan."

Feld looks at Bobby. "Perhaps we can. We'll see."

Feld goes to the door and opens it. "Thank you, Dyan."

"No, thank you, Dr. Feld, for coming. See you on Monday."

He looks at her blankly, then smiles faintly. "Oh yes, in my office."

Chapter 12

Arlene announces on the intercom, "A Mr. Ben Ari is here to see you."

"Send him in."

Diego Ben Ari smiles as he enters Feld's office. Six-feet tall, the dark and swarthy Israeli is dressed in a conservative suit. In his early fifties and well built–obviously, the man is in good shape.

"Welcome, Mr. Ben Ari, I've been expecting you. But I must admit I'm surprised you called first. Isn't usual for the Mossad to arrive unannounced?"

"Only when necessary. We can also be polite and considerate. Please call me Diego. But this visit isn't official; it's more on the order of 'informational'."

Feld points to a chair. "Please, have a seat. Can I get you something to drink?"

Ben Ari shakes his head. "No thanks, I really can't stay."

Ben Ari sits facing Feld. "First of all, I want to convey the thanks of the Israel government for all the financial and professional help that you have provided to us."

"After all, I'm a Jew and Israel's causes are my causes," Feld says pleasantly.

Ben Ari frowns. "I have to say that my visit here today is not easy."

Feld looks a little perplexed. "But important?"

"I would think it is. So I feel I must get right to the point of the visit. You're father was a survivor of Auschwitz, yes?"

Feld stiffens, then nods. "He was there four long years."

Ben Ari purses his lips. "Do you happen to know what he did there?"

"Of course, he was both an inmate and a doctor. But I'm sure you know that already."

"Do you happen to know precisely how he functioned as a doctor of the inmates?"

"I suppose so. He tried to keep the sick and injured inmates alive as long as he could."

Ben Ari falls silent, rubbing his chin.

Feld frowns. "What?"

Ben Ari sighs. "That's only partially correct."

"Look, I know that many people he treated ended up in the gas chambers anyway. Is that what you mean by 'partially correct'?"

"That, or ending up with Dr. Mengele for experimentation, or on work gangs, where they also died."

Feld shakes his head. "My God, my father was a doctor, forced to practice in the darkest recesses of hell. Do you think that was his choice? He was simply a Jew subject to the will of the Nazis, like all the inmates in Auschwitz."

"Dr. Feld, I know what inmates went through. I am not a stranger to cruelty. My father was murdered in Spain by a dictator, my mother fled to Israel where I was born. An Egyptian bomb killed her. In the '67 War, I was wounded and had to hike twenty-five miles through the desert trying to keep my intestines inside of me. I ended up in an Egyptian prison camp. True, it was not a concentration camp, but nevertheless it was hardly a pleasant place to be. So I truly understand that people do what they have to do to survive under such conditions."

Feld sighs. "What does this have to do with my father? Please, get to the point."

Ben Ari gives Feld a tolerant smile. "Your father died four years ago."

"I know that. So?"

"So–he had a Jewish burial, and this is all right."

"What are you talking about? What's 'all right'?" Feld is experienced enough to recognize that the man is struggling to impart unpleasant news.

"I'm not sure how to put this, but there is a man in Israel . . . persona non grata, an undesirable, if you will."

"I know what it means," Feld fires back impatiently.

"Of course. Anyway, my government has exiled him to the desert where he has lived for over forty years–alone. And he is no longer considered to be a Jew."

"Which means he once was a Jew? But I still don't see what this has to do with my father."

"I'm coming to that. Both this man and your father came from the same village in Germany and were in Auschwitz together. He's a physician and one of the inmate doctors that collaborated with some of the Nazi guards. He set up a form of exchange, so that when the prisoners disembarked the trains . . ."

"You mean the cattle cars, don't you?" Feld interrupts.

"Yes, the cattle cars. When they got off the cattle cars, if they had any valuables, they could insure they lived a little while longer if they gave all these possessions, like money and jewelry, to that doctor or the Nazi guards. Some gave bits of foods they had secreted on their persons. The doctor would turn all the valuables over to the guards. And there were other things done to assist the Germans."

Feld, still impatient, looks at the ceiling. "I still don't see what does this has to do with my father."

Ben Ari clears his throat. "Well, we're not absolutely sure, mind you, but we suspect this man, if he's your father, he may have assisted this inmate doctor."

Feld bolts upright in his chair. He glares at Ben Ari. "Assisted him? What the hell are you implying?"

"We think he participated in this scheme in Auschwitz. In fact, we are fairly sure of it. But, Dr. Feld, for the most part of it we are willing to let sleeping dogs lie."

Feld stands up. "Thanks for coming," he growls.

Ben Ari also gets up. He shrugs. "Because of your contributions– and the passage of time–we plan no further inquiries."

Feld slams his fist on the desk. "You bastard! No further inquiries, eh? Then why the hell did you come here in the first place? To sully my memory of my dad who worked his butt off to put me through school so I could make enough money to help support Israel; an old man who dropped dead at his sewing machine in the Garment Center?"

"We are carrying out your request that we furnish you with any information we came across about your father. It is certainly possible, Dr. Feld, that the man to whom I referred may not be your father. First of all, this man was not a doctor–and his name was different."

"Then why are you here?"

"Well, you have contributed a lot of money for a new cemetery that we will build."

"I know that."

"And you wanted a section of that cemetery dedicated to your father."

"Yes, the section reserved for the German Jews."

"Because of these questions about your father, we doubt that it is appropriate to name a section after your father."

"You said doubt, didn't you?"

Ben Ari nods. "What I mean is we will extend the benefit of the doubt to your father and not investigate any further. But we–our government–feel we owe you much and would propose to name this section of the cemetery after you."

"Thanks, but no thanks. I think I'll just decline the 'honor'."

"I am instructed by my government to advise you that because there is room for doubt, if you want your father's remains to be buried in Israel, we will, of course, find a respectable place. In any event, whatever you decide, we will return your contributions. If there is anything else you desire, do not hesitate to ask. We are in your debt."

Ben Ari hands Feld his business card and turns around to leave.

"Kept the damn money," Feld spits out. "What I want the name of that doctor in the desert."

Ben Ari sighs. "It'll do no good, I can tell you. We've questioned him for years and he admits nothing. He's old and quite ill. Trying to see him will be futile; someone did and no good came of it, just tragedy. It will be a pure waste of your time. Goodbye, Dr. Feld."

Ben Ari turns his back to Feld and reaches for the doorknob but in a few rapid strides Feld catches him, grabs his arm, and spins him around.

"It's my time and I'll waste it any way I want."

Ben Ari shakes his arm loose from Feld's grip. "We promised the old man privacy. I'll need permission from my government."

Ben Ari turns to leave, and Feld spins him around once again. "You've just got permission from me!"

Ben Ari glares angrily at Feld. "If you ever put your hands on me like that again, I'll cripple you." It wasn't said loudly but there was an explosive quality to his tone.

"And just what do you think you have now done?"

They stare at each other silently.

"Okay, Dr. Feld, you win. His name is Elias Avrams. He lives by himself in the Judean Desert not far from Jerusalem. I'll notify the proper authorities. And Dr. Feld?"

"Yes?"

"I just hope you practice more restraint with your patients." Ben

Ari straightens his jacket where Feld had grabbed it and closes the door behind him.

Feld paces around his office then flops into his desk chair. He leans his elbows on the desk, putting his head in his hands.

The intercom buzzes.

"Now what?" he snaps.

"Your next appointment, Mr. Dolan, is here and waiting," Arlene advises. He could hear a little hurt in her voice.

"Can't see him. Reschedule his appointment." He cuts off the intercom abruptly.

"Son of a bitch," he growls, jumping up and angrily swiping the papers off his desk and knocking books to the floor.

His secretary rushes in. "Dr. Feld, are you all right?"

"Yeah, I'm all right. Cancel *all* of my appointments." He doesn't look at her, but grabs his coat and rushes past Arlene and out of the office.

Chapter 13

The concierge at the King David Hotel in Jerusalem marks the spot in the desert on the map. The concierge shakes his head. "No one has lived in that part of the Judean Desert for years. It's foolish to venture into the desert without a knowledgeable escort. The nearest settlement is miles away from that spot."

Feld hands the concierge a generous tip but ignores the advice and sets out in an open Jeep. A big mistake, he quickly discovers. When not frying in the unrelenting sun, Feld seems to be swallowing half the desert sand. Squinting in the glare, he finally spots the side road that he hopes will lead him to his destination. Feld checks his map, then swerves onto to the road, barely a sand path in the desert. After about a mile, he spots a modest house, the only one he's spotted since turning onto this road. It has to be it. He pulls up, turns off the ignition, hops out, and reaches for his brief case sitting on the rear seat.

Feld raps on the door.

An old man in his eighties opens the door.

Feld puts out his hand. "I'm Dr. Bernard Feld."

Avrams grabs his hand in pulls him in. "Come in, come in, get out of the heat."

Avrams looks at his unexpected guest. "I don't know how you ended up here but if you are heading for Jerusalem, you still have a two-hour ride. I can't imagine why you're in the Judean Desert midday, but whatever the reason, you should wait to travel until the sun is low. You look a little worse for wear. Can I get you something to eat or drink? Perhaps a little iced tea?"

"Iced tea please. I must have been crazy to come here in an open jeep. I'm sure I swallowed my weight in desert sand!"

Avrams nods and pours the tea handing the glass to Feld. "Yes, the desert can be cruel, but it has its good side, you know. I've been able to grow lemons in this soil. What are you doing out here, so far from the main road? I don't get very many visitors."

Feld finishes off the iced tea in a few gulps. He did not realize how dehydrated he had become under that relentless sun. "Sorry to come unannounced, Dr. Avrams, but you have no telephone."

Avrams eyes widen. "You know my name? You've come to see *me*?"

"Surely you were expecting me, weren't you?"

Avrams chuckles. "Young man, the only visitor I'm expecting is the Messiah. Unless you're him, you're unexpected."

"That's strange. Didn't the Mossad inform you?"

"The Mossad, you say? They come once a month to bring me food and supplies. They aren't due for eight days. Why? You work for the Mossad?"

Feld smiles. "Hardly. I am just a doctor, a psychiatrist from New York. No, I'm not with the Mossad, but I do have contacts in the government."

"Feld, eh? I know that name." He shakes his right index finger. "One moment." Avrams disappears into another room and re-emerges a minute later triumphantly waving an old newspaper.

"Ah, here it is. You were the expert witness in the murder trial of the young Israeli who murdered Palestinian civilians. It seems to me there was another Feld in the news many years ago but I can't remember. Maybe it will come to me."

Avrams shakes his head. "So you convinced the court to release that criminal."

Feld nods. "Daniel Eckelman. He was insane."

"Insane, eh? I'll tell you what's insane. The whole Arab/Israeli situation is insane. You let off a murderer. If he murdered Jews, he wouldn't have been let off."

Feld sighs. He'd heard these accusations before. "Eckelman suffered from severe paranoid delusions. Moses told him to kill those Arabs; that's what he believed."

Avrams issues a short, harsh laugh. "Perhaps Moses did tell him that."

"The defense has had trouble reaching Moses for confirmation," Feld retorts.

Avrams shrugs. "Wouldn't you know it? The gods can never be found when you need them. I know, because I saw thousands die despite all the praying. Saying the *Shema* prayer didn't help. But listen, I'm sure you did not come all this way to discuss theology. What do you want with me?"

"Fair enough question. I'm here to ask about my father, Noah Feld, a doctor who lived in your village–in Germany. I believe he assisted you in Auschwitz."

Avrams rubs his chin, frowning. "Feld? I knew no such person by that name in Auschwitz."

"Perhaps by another name?" Feld asked.

The old man shakes his slowly. "There were too many other names, too many to remember."

"I can wait. I've got the time."

Avrams eyes blaze. "Well, I do not. You damn well know that I am dying. Why were you sent here? Mossad had promised me that I would not be disturbed and could die in peace. Now they send you. Why?"

"Mossad didn't send me. I'm here on my own volition."

"Then you came uninvited. Maybe you should leave."

Feld leans forward. "Dr. Avrams, I'm a psychiatrist. It is clear to me that you are carrying a very heavy burden."

"Ah, so you can read minds, too, among your other talents," Avrams says, a bitter smile on his face. "By the way, I'm just Elias Avrams, no longer 'doctor'."

Feld looks into the old man's eyes. "Sometimes I can heal minds," he says softly.

Avrams shakes his head slowly. "And you have traveled what, six thousand miles to ask me questions about things that happened over sixty years ago? Just who are you trying to heal? Yourself?"

Feld smiles. "Very perceptive, Dr. Avrams. Unfortunately, I don't have enough information to heal myself. I need your help."

"Don't speak to me, Dr. Feld. Speak to your rabbi, or perhaps, your friends in high places in Israel."

Feld sighs. "They don't have the answers I need. I think you do. I have traveled over the last ten days looking for answers. Answers that I thought I'd find in Auschwitz or in Bad Soden."

Silence. Feld sits patiently. He is used to waiting and not pushing.

Avrams leans back, his hands behind his head, looking not at Feld, but into some unfathomable distance. "Over forty years ago, Israel exiled me to this uninhabited place in the desert. They had tortured me, starved me, deprived me of water, demanded that I admit to things I did not do. I told them what I knew, but they did not want to hear it, and I continued to tell them only what I knew. Yet you come here thinking I will speak to you, tell you something different. I admire such arrogance!" Avrams stands up and turns his back on Feld.

"Now, if you will excuse me, Dr. Feld, the only thing I have to say to you is to advise you to see Jerusalem before you return to America. Walk the streets of the Old City and its venerable holy sites, then compare it to the New City. You will see, Jerusalem is magnificent."

"I'm not here as a tourist. I need your help and I believe I am in a position to help you."

Avrams turns and looks into Feld's eyes. 'Perhaps, but you are also in a position to hurt me."

"I am fully aware, Dr. Avrams, that you have requested the authorities six times to permit you to be buried among other Jews, and six times your request has been denied."

Avrams smiles. "Ah, I see. You swoop in and will supersede the local gods to have my 'defiled' body buried on sacred ground. That reminds of the returning Roman generals who, after a victory, paraded in chariots before the cheering crowds in the Coliseum. In a chariot next to the triumphant general rode another Roman, whose only function was to whisper continuously into the general's ear, 'You are not a god. You are only a man.' "

Feld brushes aside the parable. "This has nothing to do with the gods. I have contributed a great deal to Israel, both financially and professionally. The authorities are building a new cemetery for poor and unknown Jews; it will be sacred ground. There's a good chance I can convince them to bury you there."

Avrams, shrugging, sighs. "If God wills it, I will rest among my fellow Jews."

"Dr. Avrams, you said earlier, 'the gods can never be found when you need them.' So sometimes, you do need help from the outside. I think this is one of those times. Perhaps you can be the master of your own destiny, but you must decide; you can rest among the Jews or be buried among the jackals."

"I don't have long to live, you know–advanced cancer."

"I know."

"What if I die soon?"

"You will be buried among the remains of unknown Jews who are interred there. They will have room for you."

"I don't know what you expect of me; I can tell you no more than I have already told the Mossad. But let's say I do speak you. What assurance do I have that our discussions will remain confidential between us?"

"The Mishtara, the Israeli Military Police, has agreed to consider our conversations as privileged communications, much like doctor/patient. Therefore, nothing you tell me can be used against you. In fact, you can refuse to speak to me and then I must leave and that will be that because I had to agree to respect your desire for privacy. But whatever you choose, I am bound not to repeat anything you say or have said, and will not do so."

Avrams' face clouds with doubt. "Ah, I've heard that before."

Feld opens his briefcase and removes a single sheet of paper, handing it to Avrams. "Here, this is for you: a confidentiality agreement signed by me and the authorities."

Avrams examines the document and clucks. "My, you seem to wield a lot of power—quite frankly, that frightens me."

"The only power I have is my word—and I always keep it."

Avrams gets up and goes to the window. "Fifty years ago this area was mostly sand and rock. Now, there is new life; not everywhere but where there is desire, effort, and dedication. Come over here, I want to show you something."

Feld gets up and goes to the window, standing next to Avrams. Avrams points. "See that garden? It's the result of *my* efforts. Look in the distance; you can see the hills of Jerusalem, once pristine and now crowded with people. After I die, the same thing will happen here. They will come and they will build. For forty years, I have looked out this window and seen no signs of life, except for the occasional Bedouin passing through, or thieves. I try to make peace with a God whom my reason rejects, but I fight to do it. If He exists, then I want to rest with my people."

Feld puts his hand on Avrams' shoulder. "I give you my word, I will do everything I can to achieve your wish."

"I know about Auschwitz and Bad Soden. What kind of answers are you seeking? But first, tell me, about your father. Is he still alive?"

Feld shakes his head. "Two years ago, he died."

"But he must have told you something about the camp. No?"

"No, not a thing. He never spoke about it."

"Ah, not unusual. Perhaps he wanted to spare you?"

"Spare me what?"

Again, Avrams points out the window. "See that rock wall over there?"

Feld nods.

"Many years ago I started my garden, but it was not easy–a lot of rocks, some of which were very stubborn and resisted being moved. But I was just as stubborn and I dug, pushed, and prodded until they loosened. One such rock, when I could finally turn it over, had hidden a snake. The snake bit me on the hand and, being alone, I had to take out my knife, cut open my hand myself, and get the poison out. I can tell you, it wasn't easy. Since then, I've learned that some rocks are better left unturned."

Feld sighs. *Parables again*, he thought. "But look, roses bloom there now."

"Ah, my prize roses," Avrams says proudly. "My wife, God rest her soul, loved roses. But Dr. Feld, watch out for those rocks, the one you overturn my cause more pain than the one hiding the snake."

Feld grabs Avrams' hands and examines them, and then smiles. "It seems your scars are healed and your roses are blooming beautifully."

"My roses are still here, but my wife, she's buried just outside of Tel Aviv. Perhaps . . ." Avrams just shrugs.

"Perhaps what?"

Avrams withdraws his hands; he sighs. "Nothing, the subject of roses just brought on thoughts of my wife." He extends his hand. "Have a good day, Dr. Feldenstein."

"Feldenstein? Why did you call me Feldenstein? Perhaps you knew my father by the name, Noah Feldenstein?"

Avrams shrugs, but does not reply.

"Dr. Avrams, when I was twelve, my mother left and never

returned. I never knew why. I recall, as I was growing up, my father having terrible nightmares, waking up in a sweat, screaming. It scared the hell out of me but still, I would run into his room and try to comfort him. He wouldn't accept any comfort, turning away from me and telling me to leave him alone. This same man drove me mercilessly to succeed. He demanded I become a doctor, as he had been, and on his death-bed, he made me promise to fulfill *his* dream." Feld turns and walks to the window, staring out. "Now, after all that success, I have just abandoned my patients and probably destroyed my career in medicine. My wife just divorced me. She was right. I never loved her. My father chose her, because it would advance my career and I just went along with his wishes–or I should say–demands. My father drove me not only to become a doctor, but a great doctor. I achieved all this but got not even a pat on the back from him. In his last days, sometimes he did not recognize me; hadn't any idea who I was–his own son. He'd call me by the names of the dead at Auschwitz.

"Now, I have just turned my back on another woman, whom I think I love and who I think loves me. I say 'I think', because I'm not sure I know what love is or feels like; I know only ambition, competitiveness, and success.

"Dr. Avrams, you called me 'Feldenstein'. Why?"

Avrams shrugs. "Just a slip of the tongue. You said you would respect my privacy. So keep your word–and leave now, please."

Feld nods. "Dr. Avrams, I feel a deep compassion for you. I promise, before I leave for America, to see what I can do to have you rest among your people. Sorry to have bothered you."

Feld walks to the front door.

"Compassion?" Avrams says in a loud voice. "Let me tell you just what compassion is. Compassion is when you hide in a cellar with children and look into their eyes as you inject them to put them to sleep permanently so they won't fall into the hands of the Nazi butchers. It is watching poor souls brutally forced into gas chambers and seeing the pile of corpses dragged out the other end. It is not compassion, but circumstances that change people."

Feld shakes his head. "Perhaps for some people, not for me. But I suppose circumstances dictate that I leave now. I am sorry, Dr. Avrams, I hope you will forgive my intrusion."

Feld opens to the door, feeling a blast of hot desert air.

"Come back in, Dr. Feld." Avrams gestures with his arm and head towards a chair.

Feld steps back in and closes the door. He sits at a table next to Avrams.

"I worked in the camp with a Noah Feldenstein. We came from the same village of Bad Soden. The last I saw of him was when the camp was liberated and he rode out in the back of a Russian military truck."

"This Feldenstein, he must have been my father. Please, tell me about this Feldenstein."

"When I was liberated from Auschwitz, I wandered around Europe. In Hungary, I met a wonderful woman and we married. There was nothing for us in Europe after all that had happened so in 1949 we emigrated to Israel. For six years, I practiced medicine in Jerusalem, tending to the sick. One day the Mossad paid me a visit and took away my license to practice medicine. They did not arrest me and said I could stay in Israel under its laws of the Right of Return for all Jews. But they also told me I was an undesirable and suggested that I do not live among honorable Jews. What could I do? Mossad makes a suggestion only once. They spoke privately to my wife and the next thing I knew she left me. I never saw her again. As far as I can tell, she never remarried and when she died, she was buried in a grave just outside of Tel Aviv. I ended up in this house in the desert and alone. I tried to hang myself but the beam broke. I supposed it was an act of Divine Intervention. Who knows? Anyway, I decided that henceforth I would do my penance here–me, the rocks, and the sand. I worked hard and created a garden and now I have trees, vines, plants, and beautiful flowers everywhere. I shall soon see if my atonement was sufficient to please God."

"But in my experience, Dr. Avrams, it was probably the act of someone who did not want to die. After all, you're a doctor, if you really wanted to kill yourself, you would have been successful. Besides, if there is a God, I am sure he will be pleased that you helped me."

"Perhaps yes, perhaps no. I hope I can be forgiven before the cancer claims me."

Feld looks into his host's eyes. "Our prophets say one act of kindness can undo a multitude of sins."

Avrams shrugs. "Anyway, I practiced medicine in our village. In 1941, during the Christmas season, the Feldenstein family invited me to a *Shabbos* dinner at their home. Noah Feldenstein's sister was a beautiful young woman I had hoped to court. It was a clear moonlit night, sparkling with newly fallen snow. His mother was saying prayers over the candles and we were attacked by a group of Hitler Youths, who first threw a rock through the window, taunting and cursing your father's family and all Jews. Noah's father dashed outside to confront the hoodlums and he was hit with a snowball packed around a rock. He fell and the thugs beat him until he stopped moving. Noah's mother and sister rushed out to help the father and the hoodlums grabbed and started beating them also. There were too many of them, so your Noah fled out through the back of the house and into the woods."

Feld shakes his head. "My father–this Noah–left his family to die?"

"He had no choice. He could not save them and they would have killed him like they did your grandfather."

Feld bends over and covers his eyes with his hands.

"Dr. Feld, I think we've taken this far enough. Don't you think so?"

Feld picks up his head. "No, I don't think so. We have an agreement. I want to know all you know about Noah Feldenstein, my father, and what happened to my aunt and grandmother."

"I'm not continuing unless we amend the agreement."

"Excuse me?"

"There is something else I need from you."

Feld rolls his eyes. "And what's that."

"It's about my wife. I want to be buried alongside her in Tel Aviv. I need to explain to her, to apologize."

Feld shrugs. "Look, I'll do what I can. I have only so much influence, so I cannot promise."

Avrams looks at Feld through hooded eyes. "Then perhaps your money can be used to extend your influence."

"Whatever you think of me, I assure you, I'm an honest man."

"Then I have told you enough. Let the Israeli authorities fill in any other information you need. They have access to all the camp records."

"Please, Dr. Avrams, I beseech you. I doubt that my influence or money can reach that far."

"Earlier you said your power rests on the fact that you always keep your word."

"Yes, I said that and I mean it."

"Good, then give me your word right now that you will make every effort to help me *before* you leave Israel."

"You have my word."

Avrams leans back, folding his arms across his chest, staring vacantly into space. He sighs. "Sometimes, at night, I wander out in the desert and I think I can hear children crying. People have no idea what the world is like without the laughter of children." Suddenly, he straightens up and looks directly at the American psychiatrist. "But to get back to you and your interests. A German command car arrived and took the sister and the mother into custody before the Hitler Youth could finish them off and then searched the house for

Noah, but he was gone. They drove away with the two women and I never saw them again."

"What about my father, Noah?"

"Well, while I was burying your grandfather, Papa Feldenstein, your father returned from the forest. A German soldier, left there after the Gestapo had departed the scene, was watching us. 'What are you doing here?' I whispered frantically. I handed your father my medical bag, told him to sell what he could from the bag and try to get out of Germany and go to Switzerland. The soldier approached us to see what was going on and your father raced back into the forest. He was lucky he wasn't shot there and then."

"Why did you stay and bury my grandfather? Didn't they arrest you?"

Avrams shrugs. "I'm a doctor. The officers and soldiers know me. I treated them and their families for venereal diseases and for one married officer, a performed an abortion for his wife. But ultimately it did not matter, I was a Jew. The next afternoon I found myself in the railroad yard, rounded up with the rest of the Jews." He shakes his head. "It was an awful and cruel place. No food, no water, no shelter, and the guards separated families–husbands, wives, and screaming children, torn away from each other. Surprisingly, I found Noah Feldenstein there; it did not take the Gestapo long to find him. He still clutched the medical bag I had given him and the Germans, assuming he was a doctor, ordered him into the section reserved for physicians."

Feld leans forward. "Wait a minute! What do you mean 'assuming he was a doctor?' He was a doctor!"

Avrams shakes his head. "No, this Noah Feldenstein was no doctor; he was a tailor, as was his father, and his father before him."

Feld's eyes widen, disbelief etches his face; he jumps up. "A *tailor?*" He begins pacing around the room.

"I know this is a shock to you. Please, let's forget our deal and you go back to America."

"Sorry for the interruption, Dr. Avrams, please continue. I suspect this is as good a catharsis for you as for me." Feld sits down.

Once again, Avrams stares into space. Then he continues without looking at Feld. "The trip to Auschwitz in the cattle car over three days was traumatic, to say the least, but it did give me an opportunity to teach your father some basic first aid and medical terminology." Avrams now looks at Feld. "You see, the Germans needed inmate doctors and they did not check for medical degrees. You carried a medical bag, therefore you were a doctor. As simple as that."

Feld shakes his head in disbelief. "So that's how my father became a doctor?"

Avrams nods. "That's how Noah Feldenstein became a doctor. You must understand that in Auschwitz the human cargo was unloaded out of the cars onto what they call the 'ramp.' All arriving Jews were given a superficial 'medical examination', if you could call it that. Basically, it was used to not out of any concern for the Jews' health, but to determine who would be spared for slave labor or medical experimentation and who would go directly to the gas chambers."

"And my father did this culling out?" Feld asks softly.

"Yes, Noah Feldenstein did. I recall that once, during the medical processing, a woman holding a sick child broke ranks, dashing to the medical group. Feldenstein . . ."

"You mean my father."

Avrams continues as if not interrupted. ". . . Feldenstein was approached by an SS captain and asked if the child would live. Your father said yes. The officer said, 'No, I don't think so,' unholstered his pistol and shot the child in the head. The woman issued a bloodcurdling scream I can still hear today in my nightmares. She fell to the ground clutching her dead son. 'Kill me,' she shouted at the German officer, 'please, shoot me too.' The captain turned to Noah. 'Well, Dr. Juden, what about the mother? Is she fit enough to work?' Your father, in a clear voice, said, 'she is strong and will make a good worker.' The captain smiled. 'I don't think so. Tell me, Herr

Doctor, where shall I shoot her? I don't want to waste two bullets.' Your father fell silent. 'Very well, Herr Doctor, move over there,' pointing to the group headed for the gas chambers. As the officer aimed his weapon at the woman, your father broke away from the gas chamber group, rushed over, and pointed to the woman's head. 'Shoot her there,' he yelled."

"Jesus, did he do that to save his own skin or to make sure the woman didn't suffer?"

Avrams shrugs. "Who knows? Probably a little of both. Anyway, the German shot the woman and turned, aiming his pistol at your father. Suddenly, all hell broke loose. The medical commandant, a Colonel Wirths, rushed over and slapped the pistol away from the captain. 'Are you crazy?' he screamed. 'What do you think you are doing, you ignorant fool? Don't you see the medical bag? Don't you remember your orders, you ignoramus? We do not kill the doctors! I need these doctors, if not for the Jews, then to treat you and your men for syphilis and god knows what else. Now get out of here!' Wirths ordered. After the captain left with his tail between his legs, the colonel ordered your father to return to the medical group.

"Your father was never the same after that. Oh, we worked with Colonel Wirths, who exhibited some capability of kindness. He tried to convince us he was a man of conscience. Who knows? Maybe he was. Near the end of the war, he committed suicide."

Feld nods. "I guess the colonel's conscience eventually got the better of him."

Avrams shrugs. "I suppose. Do you really need to hear more, Dr. Feld?"

Feld looks into Avrams eyes. "Do you really need to tell me more? There is an old saying in my country, 'in for a dime, in for a dollar.' "

Avrams does not answer. He gets up and wanders over to the window. Looking out onto the desert, he continues. "I requested your father to be my assistant. We worked together at Auschwitz for almost four years. I kept teaching him basic medicine and as he became proficient he was assigned with me to the 'ramp,' where we selected the ones who were fit to go on work details."

"And your decision on others, Dr. Avrams? To the gas chambers?" asks Feld, a trace of quiver in his voice.

Avrams nods. "Either do that or end up assisting Doctor Mengele in medical experimentation."

Feld straightens up in his chair, takes a deep breath. "Mengele? Did you say Mengele? The notorious Dr. Mengele? The Angel of Death?"

Avrams doesn't seem to hear the questions, but instead continues his monologue. He moves back to his chair. "At the 'ramp', often new arrivals would offer us food or other things, other valuables, in exchange for . . ." His voice trails off. He looks at Feld, almost beseechingly. "We were no different than anyone else at the camp."

"Except for the six million who died," Feld says with a little more anger than he intended. "Tell me, Dr. Avrams, did my father take food from these poor souls?"

"Like the others in the camp, he was starving. He did what he had to, to survive."

The words feel like a hard slap, Feld's anger rises up. He tries to control it but without much success. "But you *did* survive! Tell me, doctor, how does it feel?"

Avrams sighs. "You have to ask?"

"All I know is that my father toiled all his life in America sewing buttons on women's coats in a small cubicle in the Garment Center in New York City. He didn't tell me he wasn't a doctor before he went to Auschwitz; only that he couldn't afford the medical training necessary to get his license to practice in America." Feld bends over and puts his head in his hands. "He told me he was saving for me to become a doctor like him. But, Dr. Avrams, damn it, I never wanted to become a doctor!"

"Your father didn't want to be a doctor either, but he saw it as a way to survive, and he did survive. I'm certain he saw that as a way for you to survive as well."

Feld flinches. The blood seems to drain from his face. "Survive? Is that what you call it? *He* decided who would live, who would die. He took *their food*. He had a choice, Dr. Avrams, he had a choice . . ." His voice trails off.

The two men look at each other. Finally Feld speaks. "I'm afraid to ask the question, but tell me Dr. Avrams, did my father do any work with Dr. Mengele?"

Avrams shrugs. "You think we had a choice? You think facing the gas chambers and ovens or surviving is a choice? If you do, then you simply don't understand inmate behavior, not withstanding your impressive credentials as a psychiatrist."

Feld nods. "Tell me, what did my father do in the Mengele experiments?"

"No, I will not and cannot go into that. You ask too much of me and the other inmate doctors. Just let me say, Dr. Feld, your father was not a monster. In time, I hope you will forgive him. Perhaps you will come to understand that your father was also in a group that dedicated itself to the care of others. The same thing you do now in your profession. And that is a good thing, no? Well, your father also did good in the camp. He healed sick workers that prevented sending them to the gas chambers. He saved many of the lives of people who would have died if he wasn't there ministering to them. And most of those who did die would have died anyway."

Feld shakes his head. "I can't believe you are trying to justify the worst kind of cowardice and participation in selective murder and torture."

"The group that survived did so thanks in part to your father and *that* group had hope for the future. Can you see that? They thought about what they would do when they were liberated. It kept them going under the cruelest of circumstances." Avrams smiles sardonically. "Even now, I have a hope for the future. I hope to be buried among my people, next to my wife."

"I already told you, if it's possible, it will happen."

Avrams continues, not acknowledging Feld's last comment. "There was also another group of inmates that most of us avoided. The ones that gave up hope and in so doing died within themselves. Some mornings, you'd try to wake these people and one or more of them would be dead. You said earlier that your father had a choice. Maybe he did. But you have a choice too, whether you like it or not. You can wither away and die within yourself, or you can be grateful for the life you have and go home and repair the damage you have done to yourself in your profession. It's a fine profession and you are a good doctor. So instead of engaging in self-pity as you are doing now, go back to America and continue to do good. You mentioned a woman who loves you. You are lucky. I miss my wife, as I am sure you miss your father. Go back to your woman friend and find out if there is a life for you with her. Don't wait until she's in her grave."

Avrams eyes widen. "Ah, I knew it would come to me. I remember the other Feld. There was a Miriam Feld who was killed on that very road you just come in on. Undoubtedly, she must be related to you."

Feld bolts upright. "Wait a minute. Miriam Feld is my mother!"

"Of course, I should have known. I'm sorry."

"You said my mother was dead. How did that happen?"

Avrams purses his lips. "I recall that an American, Miriam Feld and the Mossad man driving her, died when a roadside bomb planted by some Palestinian terrorists destroyed the car, just a few miles from here. It was in all of the papers. Now it falls into place for me. You mean you didn't know your mother was killed?"

Feld leans back in the chair looking up at the ceiling. He runs his hands through his hair. "No," he says softly, "I didn't know. What was she doing with the Mossad?"

"I can only suppose he was taking her to see me. I'm sorry to be the bearer of such bad news. But it was in all the Israeli newspapers, though they didn't identify the man as from the Mossad. But I knew; I recognized the name. Once again, I apologize for dropping this on you in such a manner."

"No, I don't fault you, Dr. Avrams; it just comes as such a shock. But I do appreciate you telling me. Thank you."

Avrams gets up and pours himself a drink of water. "Have to keep hydrated in the desert. Look, Dr. Feld, I've had a long day and I am exhausted. Wait until it gets dark, and you won't get lost. Just follow the distant glow–that will be Jerusalem."

Avrams puts his hand on the shoulder of the still-sitting Feld. "It's your turn, Dr. Feld; it is you standing at the 'ramp', just as your father did and just as I did. Now you know more than the Mossad– not many people can say that. And now you can decide my fate."

Feld gets up and faces the old man. "No sir, not me, Dr. Avrams, I'll not be the instrument of your judgment. That'll be up to the God that you may have finally found and whom you fear."

"It is possible, Dr. Feld, I was wrong about God. I've lived forty years in this desert in exile. Because just as I am about to die, he sends me a prophet to finally bring me rest."

Feld starts toward the door. He turns to face Avrams. "Perhaps you'll just have to explain to this God why you took his job at Auschwitz."

Avrams shrugs. "Death, Dr. Feld, is simply a shadow that follows all of us. It can descend quickly or very slowly–and we never know. So bury the dead who haunt your heart and mind." He sighs. "If you don't, they'll outlive you."

Feld opens the door and looks back. "I promised you I would speak to my contacts in Jerusalem and I will. I'll let you know what they say."

"One moment, if you please." Avrams moves over to the other side of the room and picks up a plant. "Here, take this," handing the plant to Feld. "It's a sabra. You know what that means don't you?"

Feld nods. "Born in Israel."

"Exactly. It's very coarse on the outside but when you take a careful look on the inside, you will discover much goodness. Sometimes, Dr. Feld, you have to look deeply into a person to discover the goodness within. Don't forget that. Shalom, Dr. Feld. Have a safe journey."

Feld steps out into the desert heat, then turns around before closing the door. He looks at Avrams and smiles. "Shalom, Dr. Avrams."

Chapter 14

Feld drops into his first-class seat in the El Al Boeing 747 aircraft. He shakes his head in wonderment at the security procedures of the Israeli airline. Three hours in the terminal with three different sets of security people asking questions on the ownership of his luggage, whether he packed them himself, whom he spoke to in the terminal and why–it seems that someone had watched him strike up a conversation over a cup of coffee in the terminal snack shop. But he knew he wasn't singled out for special treatment; he noticed that security subjected almost every passenger to similar treatment. He'd read somewhere that Pan Am had studied the El Al system and decided it was too expensive and intrusive. Shortly after that decision, a Pan Am flight blew up over Lockerbie, Scotland. He'd heard that El Al put four or five armed undercover agents on every overseas flight. Well, the security was a hassle, but it certainly gives him peace of mind.

The flight attendant brings him a dry martini in a single serving bottle. He pours it into the glass and settles back into the comfortable leather seat. He tries to nod off but his mind is too active and agitated, even after finishing the martini. He leafs through the El Al magazine and the tax-free shopping brochure–nothing interests him.

He keeps turning over in his mind the meeting with Avrams. *There was so much more I could have asked him–perhaps best I did not.*

I gave up everything to find the truth and now that I have it–or at least a good part of it–does it make me any happier? Hardly, for to be told that the father I loved–the father that sacrificed for me–had been a monster is, for me, a crushing revelation. Perhaps even worse, father lied to me about my mother, leading me to believe she had abandoned us. Avrams and I talked about catharsis. Well, perhaps it's there for me, but the thing about catharsis is that often only the future will reveal its effect–good, bad, or indifferent. Ha! My patients should only hear me now!

When asked if my father worked with Dr. Mengele, Avrams replied, "You think we had a choice?" Simple words in response, but with implications that were absolutely crushing.

Just as soon as Feld returned to the hotel in Jerusalem, he researched concentration camp medical experimentation. Having access to a computer and a printer in the hotel business office, a typical perk found in high-end accommodations, Feld googled "Dr. Mengele" and came up with a wealth of facts on the doctor's activities at Auschwitz–really too much information to be wholly digested. And for a doctor weaned on the ethics of medicine, to Feld, it read like the ultimate horror and nightmare story, a tale of a profession gone absolutely stark-raving mad–the Frankenstein of the real world.

He reaches down for his business case, parked under the space of the seat in front of him and pulls out several printouts from material he'd flagged and printed out during his computer search–principally on medical experimentation in Auschwitz, mostly occurring in 1944 and some in 1945.

He selects one of the printouts on Dr. Mengele and reviews some of the text he'd highlighted. The medical facility in Auschwitz, it seems, was under the command of a Dr. Eduard Wirths, the same officer who Avrams said saved my father from being shot by the SS captain. Wirths oversaw various experiments on inmates to help German combat troops in their treatment and recovery from the physical wounds of war and from the mental trauma of combat, to assist in the development of new weapons to incapacitate the enemy, and to support Hitler's racial dogmas. But the experiments themselves were carried out under the prime responsibility of University of Munich Medical College graduate, Dr. Josef Mengele–and the doctor did so with relish and a perverse dedication. His most infamous experiments were on twins. He had scoured the unloading docks for twin children to carry out grotesque genetic experiments. He'd inject a variety of substances into their eyes to see if he could change the color of their eyes, a part of their genetic makeup; many were blinded or died from infection. It is said he kept a display case of such twins' eyeballs. Some twins he joined–literally–by sewing them together on the operating table–none survived. He removed the organs of twins, while they were alive and often without anesthesia, to compare them. He injected twins with disease to see how quickly each would succumb.

Experiments weren't limited to twins, by any means. He conducted studies on the treatment of hypothermia for the *Luftwaffe* by immersing inmates, adult males, in tanks of ice water for up to five hours at a time, or kept them outside naked in below-freezing weather, then experimented on different ways of rewarming those that had survived the ordeal. Hundreds perished in these experiments or were simply murdered after the experiment concluded. Other inmates were deliberately exposed to mustard and other poisonous gasses that inflicted horrible injuries so that Mengele could assess the most effective treatment. He injected still others with diseases like malaria, tetanus, streptococcus, and even an agent to cause gangrene. Some unlucky inmates were forced to live on a diet of seawater; others were sterilized or secretly fed poisoned food, then killed to perform autopsies. Mengele inflicted horrible burns with phosphorus substances used in incendiary bombs in order to prepare pharmaceutical preparations to treat similar burns on German soldiers. Many inmates died from the experiments themselves and others were murdered in order to perform autopsies. Still others were exterminated when no longer useful for experimentation.

Feld sighs, putting down the printout in his lap. The atrocities go on and on, but he's read enough. Avrams did not specifically spell out what my father actually did in Mengele's ward, but Avrams' body language spoke volumes, as did Feld's own imagination. Back in Jerusalem, he'd forced himself to read the entire Google output in order to understand the magnitude of what had been done, and appreciate the part, however small, his father must have played in this horror. There was no getting away from it–his father posed as a doctor for all the years in Auschwitz to survive, and assisted in Mengele's experiments in order to live yet another day in the concentration camp while others died, some horribly.

Well, I asked for it and Avrams hit me square between the eyes. Now the question is what am I going to do with the knowledge? Go forward and make a life for myself or, as Dr. Avrams put it, wallow in self-pity? The facile answer seems obvious, but will my mind permit to make that choice? It was a question he had posed to patients too many times to count, but only now could he appreciate the difficulties in taking the path that moved forward.

Why did my father lie to me up until the end that he was a doctor? Did he think I'd love him any the less if he was a tailor in the old country? And he used that lie to force me into medicine. Should I thank him or curse him for that? Perhaps the shame of his actions posing as a doctor was so great that he felt he had no choice. Possibly, I could understand that, but the lies about my mother abandoning me when in fact she was killed by a roadside bomb while riding in an automobile in Israel, that's unforgiveable.

Feld picks up another printout, but not on Mengele. He peruses a news report in the Jerusalem Post, English edition, of the roadside bomb that killed two on the desert road just outside of Jerusalem. Two people were killed, the article reported, the driver of the automobile and his passenger. The passenger had been identified as Miriam Feld from Brooklyn, New York. Her next of kin had been notified. No mention was made that the driver was with Mossad. A commentary in the Post, a few days later, asked when the army was going to crack down on terrorists that caused such carnage.

Another article reported that Miriam Feld had been buried in a small cemetery in Jerusalem.

How many years had I blamed myself for her leaving, trying to fathom what I had done to drive her away and assumed on my young shoulders that heavy burden of guilt? How much has my father screwed up my relationships with women leaving me with a deep fear of abandonment by them and of being left alone once again? Instead of becoming a baseball outfielder, he turned me into social outsider.

Feld knew that mother had also been a survivor of the concentration camps; that she had met father when they were DPs in Europe, emigrated to the United States together and married. *She must have known what was going on in the camp and she knew, or, I should say, thought my father was a doctor in that camp. What suspicions were aroused in her? When? Only now, after speaking to Dr. Avrams, could he begin to deduce from the newly learned facts the reasons for her trip abroad. Of course! At some point, she knew that her husband was not merely an innocent survivor of the Holocaust. And she went abroad to find the answers. Why else go to only Germany and Israel?*

Where else could she find the information she needed, but those two countries? She searching for the same information that I just unearthed in the Israeli desert! That's why she tried to see Dr. Avrams! Now I'm sure she was going to return home, never intending to abandon me. She told me, before she left, that she was going to Germany and Israel and I just buried it in my subconscious.

At least I kept my promise to Avram by doing my best to convince the Israeli authorities to reverse their decision on his burial. I pointed out the unfairness of singling out him among the hundreds of doctors forced to do some of the same things under those horrible circumstances, circumstances that one who was not there could not possibly understand or appreciate. They agreed to reconsider their decision. That was the most I could hope for at this time.

The El Al 747 takes off from Ben Gurion International Airport bound for JFK in New York. Feld looks out at the receding lights of

Tel Aviv, known as the Mediterranean metropolis that never sleeps. A city he only taxied through without really seeing during his one-track mission.

He wonders, could ever sleep? Feld lowers his seatback to the reclining position and tries, but his own demons take over, those of his shattered practice, stranded patients, and the loss of the one woman who might have made his life whole again–and her disappointed son still waiting for his promised baseball game at Yankee Stadium.

After a little under an hour of restlessness, he raises his seatback to the upright position, returns the printouts to his business case, and orders another dry martini with an olive. He recalls having a professor who wisely hung this sign over his desk. "Oh, Lord, teach me when to let go."

It was going to be a long, long flight home.

Chapter 15

Feld paces his office restlessly, deep in thought. He worries about how his former receptionist, Arlene, whom he left in the lurch when he took off unannounced for Israel, would react. If she spit in his eye, he'd not blame her. A knock on the door startles him.

"Come on in, the door's open."

He watches Arlene enter.

"Hello, Dr. Feld."

He walks over to her and puts a hand on her shoulder. "Arlene, it's good to see you." He motions to a chair. "Have a seat. It's nice of you to come over. I do appreciate it." He sits facing her.

"Look, doctor, I'm on my lunch break, so I only have a half-hour, at most."

"I understand, so I'll get right to the point. How do you like working for Dr. Perkins?"

She shrugs. "Oh, it took me a while to get used to his British accent and the pipe he smokes, but it's okay, I suppose."

"He's a fine doctor. In that sense, you're fortunate. How did you get the position?"

"Oh, he ran an ad in the *New York Times*. I called him and I told him I had been your receptionist for well on four years." Arlene smiled. "He hired right on the phone, without an interview. He asked me how you were doing and why I was leaving your employ.

What could I tell him? I certainly didn't know. So I said you were taking a sabbatical and that I needed a full-time job."

Feld flinches. "Arlene, I'm afraid I owe you an apology."

She stares at him in bewilderment. "Yes, you do, and I'm not the only one, you know. You have a lot of patients, very angry ones who didn't know where you were, or why you left. They expected me to tell them, but I hadn't any idea. I really didn't know what to do; it was embarrassing. I stayed for two weeks after you stormed out, but I just couldn't continue. I've got a mortgage and two kids to feed."

Feld leans back in his chair, crossing his arms over his chest. "Yes, I understand."

She falls silent. Feld gets up and goes to his desk, opening the top drawer. He withdraws an envelope with her name on it. He hands it to her.

"This is the pay I owe you, plus a month's severance."

Arlene shakes her head. "I can't accept severance pay because I found a job right away. I don't know what to say."

"I insist you take the severance. You deserve it."

She hikes her eyebrows. "Now, I'm the one feeling guilt. Just like *I* deserted *you*."

Feld grows maudlin. He sighs. "No, Arlene I deserted not only you but my patients . . . and even myself. You were a real asset to me and I'm very sorry to have lost you."

"Before I left, I forwarded all you telephone messages to your service. Most of them were simply asking where you were and when would you be back. But two messages you should know about. Mrs. Gaffney and Mr. Gold are threatening to start a class action against you for malpractice."

He smiles. "In a way that's good. Considering I've been trying to get those two to participate in group activities for years! Oh, I'll give them a few free sessions and we can probably settle this without going to court." Feld hesitates.

Arlene could sense it. "Yes? Anything else?"

Feld rubs his chin. "Did Dyan Regan call?"

Arlene nods. "Two or three times. Plus her son Bobby came up to the office–the first time to confirm that you were taking him to a baseball game. Later, he came back with a bag full of the presents you had given him–a lot of baseball stuff. He said to tell you he didn't want them anymore. I put the bag under your desk."

Feld sits down and reaches under his desk. Shaking his head, he pulls out the bag. He grabs the baseball glove, pounding his fist into its pocket. "Christ, I spent two years building up trust between his mother and me and in just two weeks, I tore it all down. What a doctor I am!"

Arlene shrugs. "I'm not so sure. I think if you apologize to Dyan Regan and bring the presents back to Bobby and perhaps take him to a ballgame, things will work out fine. People can be a lot more understanding than you think."

Feld looks at her more closely. "Understanding, perhaps. Forgiving, that's another kettle of fish altogether. It comes from a different place."

"Then perhaps first *you* could find that place and forgive yourself. I know you're a good man, Dr. Feld."

He laughs. "You practicing without a license? Maybe I should lie on this couch and pay you."

She swallows hard, looking down. "I'm sorry, Dr. Feld, truly I am for speaking out of turn."

He gets up from his desk and sits down next to her. He places his hand gently on her arm. "You weren't out of turn, Arlene. It's me, I'm out of turn, and I have been for my whole life."

She stands up, looking down on Feld. "I'm sorry but I have to get back to work. Dr. Perkins will be wondering where I am."

Feld rises off the couch and faces Arlene. "Is there any chance of winning you back? Look, I'll give you a raise. Of course, I'll give you all the time you need to find a replacement for Dr. Perkins."

"It's tempting, but I've been working for Dr. Perkins for only a few days."

Feld sighs. "You were with me for a few years."

Arlene puts her hands on her hips. "Can I be perfectly honest with you, Dr. Feld?"

"Of course."

"For four years I worked for you and found you to be the most professional person I ever met. To tell you the truth, it scared me to death. When I first started, I half expected to be fired at any time. I got those silent messages you sent warning me to toe the line. But I stayed and was very comfortable working for you. I really enjoyed it. Then boom, you storm out of here last month without explanation; you don't tell a living soul where you're going or how to get in touch with you. I really thought you had a nervous breakdown and I just don't know now whether you're the same person. I could leave another good job, come back, and poof you're gone again."

"You're absolutely right and I'm sorry, truly sorry. Look, something just exploded inside of me and I had to go looking for the missing pieces. Now I'm trying to reassemble those pieces."

He walks to the office door and opens it. "I realize you're late and I'm sorry I kept you here so long. Your work here has been superb and you were very important to my practice."

Arlene gets up and heads for the door. Half out the door, she stops and turns. "As long as we're being honest with each other, I must tell you that I'm not very happy at my new job. Dr. Perkins, I'm afraid, is quite stuffy and boring, wearing those tweed jackets with leather elbow patches and constantly smoking that damn pipe. The entire office area, including reception, stinks from the smoke. I come home every evening smelling like a bar patron. He even smokes it in the bathroom!"

Feld grins. "Well, I wear solid suits and my office is still a smoke-free environment."

She puts her hand up in front of her mouth and whispers

conspiratorially, "His patients tell me he falls asleep during the sessions."

"It's undoubtedly something in his pipe."

"That crossed my mind."

Both of them share a good laugh.

"Arlene, how much is Perkins paying you?"

She puts on a smug face. "Oh, twenty-five dollars more a week than you did."

He shakes his index finger in the air. "I'll give you thirty-five dollars more."

She smiles easily. "I'll have to think on it."

He slaps his head in mock frustration. "And you can have another week's vacation."

"Oooh, that is tempting, very tempting. I'll have to let you know."

He rubs his chin. "And you can keep the severance pay."

Arlene shakes her head. "I just couldn't."

"Force yourself."

She spreads her arms in surrender. "I guess that's an offer I can't refuse. I'll be here a week from Monday. In the meantime, I'll see that you have a temp to fill in."

"I have a better idea. Why don't you get *Dr. Perkins* the temp and," pointing directly at her, "you start here on Monday."

"I'll let you know." Arlene walks over to his desk and tosses the severance envelop down on it and walks out the door. She pauses. "You know you can't do everything with money."

He shrugs and goes back to his desk.

A few seconds later, Arlene pokes her head in the door, grinning widely. "What time Monday?"

"Eight-thirty?"

"How about nine o'clock!"

Feld shakes his head. "You drive a hard bargain."

"But I'm worth it and you know it."

"Agreed."

Arlene gives a little nod. "See you Monday. Meanwhile use that severance money to take the Regan boy to the ballpark."

Feld waves her away as she leaves the office. He sits at his desk, contacts his service, and listens to his first telephone messages.

"This is Judge Hollaran and . . ."

He finishes listening, bends over, and picks of the bag of presents Bobby returned. He gets up with the package in hand and heads out of the office. He stops, turns back, and picks up the baseball sitting in a holder on his credenza. He dusts it off, rubs it, and places it in his pants pocket.

Then he returns to his desk and dials a number. He hears Saul Edelman's voice at the other end of the line.

"Hello?"

"Saul? This is Bernie Feld."

"Bernie? What the hell happened to you? You failed to show up at the meeting with the hospital board. We tried to contact you and couldn't. To say the board was pissed in a gross understatement. They gave the job to Ed Loury."

"I'm really sorry Bernie."

"Sorry? I broke my ass to get you that position."

"I feel bad I got egg on your face before the board."

"Egg, hell. It was an entire Waldorf breakfast. I hope you didn't quit psychiatry and become a Little League coach."

"Saul, I need to see you professionally–as a patient. Will you do it?"

"Well . . . I would like to close your file."

"I'd like to bring someone with me."

"If it's Susan, I'll do it *pro bono*."

"No, Saul, it's not Susan, it's my father."

Silence on the other end.

"Oh, come on, Saul. How's ten tomorrow morning fit into your schedule?"

Saul sighs. "See you then, I guess."

"Thanks, Saul."

Feld hangs up the phone, picks up his package, and heads out the door.

Chapter 16

This time he has no trouble finding her building or apartment. He rings the doorbell. He could see someone looking at him through the fisheye peephole in the door. Regan opens the door and Feld just stands there, bag dangling in hand, waiting. "Dr. Feld, please come in. I was just about to file a missing persons report with the police."

Feld crosses the threshold, standing in the foyer. "I came to talk to you," he says softly.

"Talk?" she repeats.

Feld nods. "Also, I want to return these presents to Bobby. He left them at my office with instructions 'never to buy him anything again.' "

She smiles and takes the bag. "I just wish he'd give me those exact same instructions."

She glances inside the bag, then looks at him closely, her eyes locking onto his. "Where the hell have you been? What did you do? Go visit the Dalai Lama?"

He shrugs. "Research, I had to do some research."

"Research?" she echoes.

"Just some personal research and a lot of soul-searching."

"Did you ever consider just how unprofessional you acted in deserting your patients with nary a peep of explanation?"

"I am truly sorry."

"And did your 'soul-searching' lead to at least some enlightenment, I hope?"

"Yes."

Regan folds her arms across her chest. "Okaaay, we got that out of the way. Now, what exactly can I do for you?"

"Talk, I need to talk to you."

"As my doctor or as an enlightened lost soul-searcher?" she asks, struggling not to let too much sarcasm creep into her tone.

"Only as me, Dyan," he says softly. "Only as me, as best I can."

Her face becomes grave and her body very still. "Do your best, doctor. Would it be easier if you lie on the couch?"

He ignores the ill-concealed barb. "Dyan, I'm terminating your therapy with me."

Now anger creeps into her voice. "Oh, really, I had no idea. Somehow, I just supposed you were gone for two weeks secretly to prepare another inkblot test for me."

Feld, out of the corner of his eye, sees Bobby standing quietly at the door to the room.

"Look, Dyan, want to be honest with you and explain why I'm terminating the treatment."

She shakes her head vigorously. "Really, Dr. Feld, it's not necessary–I dismissed you two weeks ago. Next Wednesday, I'm starting with a new therapist." Anger wells up in her. "Now just leave and take these with you," handing him the bag of gifts for Bobby.

Feld just stands there, holding the bag at his side.

"I don't know your feelings for my little Bobby, but I won't let you run him up and down like a yoyo–or for that matter, run me also–whenever it pleases you."

"Dyan, listen to me. I can't continue with your therapy because of my personal feelings for you. They get in the way."

"Did you say 'your personal feelings'? What about me? About *my* personal feelings?"

He looks up at the ceiling, rubbing his forehead. *God, how do I get through to her?* "You must hear what I'm saying now, Dyan. I am going through a divorce. It's making me lonely and frightened. I feel like my whole life has been a lie."

She glares at him aggressively, hands on hips. "I see. You came here to tell me some more lies. Son-of- a . . ." She stops in mid-sentence when she remembers Bobby is within earshot but her emotions start to get the better of her and she continues. "You made me face my monsters, you know. Why don't you have the balls to face your own?" She laughs harshly. "Isn't that something? 'Balls,' that's a pretty good baseball metaphor." She spreads her arms wide in frustration. "Oh, why don't you just grow up?"

His eyes have that sad look. "The problem, Dyan, is I think I am in love with you. That's why I can't continue with your therapy."

Dyan sobs, shaking her head violently. "God, you're a lunatic. They should take away your license to practice."

Feld just stands there, saying nothing. Silence hangs over them for several seconds.

Regan presses her lips together. "In your office," she says softly, "I sat on the couch and you listened to all the intimate and sordid details of my life. I let you into my head, into my life. I watched your eyes, and listened to the tone of your voice for some sign that I am something more than a laboratory guinea pig. You put me back into my past life, into that hell, then you patted my hand, gave me a gold star, and told me, 'nice job'. Then you disappear for weeks without a single word, come back with this crap that you want to stop my therapy because you 'think' you are in love with me. Know what I think? I think you're a crazy, crazy man; you're sick!"

He shrugs. "I lived my own life, pretending to help people with their lives by facing their problems. Why? Because I was simply too frightened to face my own. Things started to change when I met you and Bobby. You must believe that," he says plaintively.

Regan takes a deep breath. "Mm, I understand. Why don't you just give me a call, in say, a hundred years?"

"No, you don't understand. I loved baseball with a passion, ever since I was a little boy. You know what my dream was? To grow up to be a major league player." Feld shakes his head. "I never wanted to be a doctor, never. But a doctor I became because that was what my father so desperately wanted." He paused, looking down at his shoes. Now he speaks almost in a whisper. "My mom? When I was twelve, she up and left. My father led me to believe she abandoned us, or more specifically, abandoned *me*. I had that pain with me all my life. But I buried it. It must have been my fault, I agonized. What did I do wrong to force her to leave? Why didn't she love me enough to stay–like you love Bobby? I found out later that she didn't leave, that she died in a car in Israel. My father knew and never told me. Worse, he led me to believe otherwise."

She unfolds her arms. "I'm truly sorry," she replies with an empathy she hadn't shown–or felt– before.

Feld nods. "My father was at Auschwitz. He told me he saved lives. But I just found out he lied. In fact, he did terrible things. It almost destroyed him. Subconsciously at least, I knew this was a damaged and troubled human being. But he was the only one I had and I loved him. When he was in the hospital dying, I asked him if there was anything I could do. He looked at me with those frightened hollow eyes and shook his head. So I decided, this once, to give him a treat. I went to the hospital cafeteria and bought him an ice cream sandwich–just a plain old ice cream sandwich that most people take for granted and enjoy all their lives. When he tasted it, his eyes lit up, like I've never seen before. He smiled broadly and for a moment I saw something new–delight on his face. Then I realized that he probably never had ice cream. He had to be a day away from death before he tasted it! That's when I thought, how much of life did this poor old man deny himself?"

Regan sighs. "And what about you? How much of life did you deny yourself?"

He looks down, not answering the question. Then his face brightened. "I do have some good news."

Regan's eyes widen. "What?"

"I had a message from the court on my answering machine. It seems that the police arrested your ex-husband, charging him with assaulting his wife. You know what that means don't you? With my report, Judge Halloran says he will grant you full and permanent custody of Bobby!"

Regan laughs harshly, shaking her head. "After your disappearing act, you think the court will accept *your* recommendation?"

Feld smiles. "Not to worry, I told the court I took a personal sabbatical."

"Dr. Feld?"

He turns to the voice and sees Bobby walking toward him.

"Hi, Bobby," Feld says with an enthusiasm he truly felt.

Bobby bows his head. "You missed the baseball game," he says reproachfully but softly.

Feld shuffles his feet. "Yes, I know. Something important came up and I had to go away. I'm really sorry. I should have called you."

Bobby pauses, seeming to pick his words carefully. "Mom says . . ."

"What, Bobby? What does she say? You can tell me."

". . . that you were a coward," he blurts out.

Feld nods slowly. "She's absolutely right, Bobby. And I'm really sorry you won't keep the gifts."

"Nah, I don't want them." Again, Bobby pauses, struggling with himself. "Besides," he says quickly, "my mother won't let me keep them."

Feld smiles. "Bobby, you have a good mother. You should listen to her."

Feld reaches for the handle of the front door. "See you around, buddy. Okay?" He starts to walk out.

Feld stops and turns around. He reaches in his pants pocket, having a little trouble extracting the item. Finally, he produces the baseball. He looks at Regan for approval then turns to Bobby and, bending to the boy's height, extends his hand holding out the baseball. "Bobby, would you at least take this. My mother gave me this baseball when I was about your age, perhaps just a little older."

Bobby doesn't reach out for the ball, but does look at it lightly held on Feld's fingertips. Bobby's eyes widen. "Hey, neat! This ball is signed by the Yankee Clipper, Joe DiMaggio!"

Feld shrugs. "What can you do? The Dodgers had already moved to Los Angeles and I could get only a *Yankee* to sign it. What do you think?"

"Yeah, I like the Yankees." Feld tosses the ball into Bobby's hands.

Bobby looks into Feld's eyes. "Why are you a coward?"

"A fair question, Bobby. It's because I did not have the courage to do or at least to try to do in my life what I really wanted."

Bobby's face lights up with understanding. "Like play baseball? You really wanted to play, didn't you?"

"Yeah, Bobby. That plus love people and let them love me."

Bobby looks up at Feld. "I want to come with you."

Feld shakes his head sadly. "I'm afraid you can't."

Bobby becomes agitated, stamping his foot. "But *you* said we were friends. Dr. Feld, I *really* wanted those gifts, but my mother wouldn't let me have them."

Feld puts a gentle hand on Bobby's shoulder, speaking softly. "First and foremost, Bobby, you've got to listen to you mother."

"But you said you should do what you *want* to do, didn't you?"

"But in this case you listen to your mother. She wants and knows what is best for you."

Bobby, on the verge of tears, blurts out, "But if you go now, I'll never, ever see you again."

Feld presses his lips together. "Oh, we'll keep in touch and perhaps take in a ballgame."

Bobby whirls around to face his mother. "Mom, can we go to a baseball game, can we?"

Feld looks at Regan with raised eyebrows.

Regan jostles Bobby's hair. "We'll get together. I'll take you. Now take the presents and thank Dr. Feld. He has to go. He has a lot to do."

Bobby turns to Feld. "Do you like my mom?"

Out of the mouth of babes, Feld thinks. "Yes I do, very much."

Feld looks at Regan, their eyes lock for a split second.

Feld again starts toward the door. "Well, I'm afraid I have to go now."

Bobby runs to the door, blocking Feld's exit.

Regan moves to Bobby, standing behind him, her hands resting on his shoulders.

She sighs. "Bobby and I have had enough instability in our lives," she says quietly and looks at Feld, her eyes tearing up.

"I'm starting therapy next Monday," Feld announces.

Bobby continues to press. "My mom likes you, Dr. Feld. I know because she told me so."

Feld laughs. "You know Bobby, you can be a very brash little boy sometimes, yes, sir."

"That's because I don't have a father to teach me."

Regan smiles. "And it looks like your chances of obtaining one are getting slimmer by the minute."

Regan laughs out loud, Feld and Bobby join in.

Feld turns to Regan. "Listen, the Yankees play the Baltimore Orioles next Sunday. Can I take Bobby?"

Regan's eyes narrow. "I thought you don't like the Yankees."

Feld shrugs. "It's certainly easier than going to Los Angeles for the afternoon, isn't it?"

Regan puts her hands on her hips confrontationally. "I just don't know, Dr. Feld, whether I can trust you with Bobby. You could disappear and leave him stranded in the ballpark."

Feld smiles. "Well, then why don't you just come with us? Perhaps we can have dinner after the ballgame?"

Regan continues to challenge Feld. "What if you don't show up–again?"

"Don't worry, I'll show up."

Regan looks down at Bobby. "What do you think, should we give this Brooklyn Bomb another chance?"

"Bum," Feld corrects.

"Excuse me?"

"They were called 'Brooklyn Bums', not the 'Brooklyn Bombs'."

Regan pretends to be huffy. "Huh, that's probably more appropriate."

Bobby jumps up and down. "All right!" he yells. He races to the bag of presents and pulls out the baseball glove. He reads the inscription on the heel of the glove. "Johnny Podres," he says out loud. "Who's he?"

Regan moves over to Feld, squeezing his hand. He returns the gesture. Their eyes meet.

Bobby smiles, not missing a thing.

* * *

Fans, it's a great day at Yankee Stadium; a large crowd is enjoying the sunshine on this fine day. The Orioles leadoff batter steps up to the plate. There's the familiar cry of "play ball" as a warm breeze blows towards the outfield.

About the Authors

Carl Steinhouse, a retired lawyer, was a federal prosecutor for the United States Department of Justice for 15 years after which he went into private practice specializing in class actions, white-collar crime, and civil and criminal trials. In the early fifties, he served as an intelligence analyst in the Army Counterintelligence Corps.

Mr. Steinhouse was Vice Chairman of the Antitrust Section of the American Bar Association, and on the editorial boards of two Bureau of National Affairs publications. He also wrote and edited books on grand jury practice, criminal trial practice, and criminal juries and a frequent lecturer at ABA National Institutes and video courses on grand jury and criminal trial practice. He is a frequent contributor to the Naples Daily News writing about the humorous side of the law.

In the 80's and 90s he was active on an international level for the National Conference on Soviet Jewry, making several trips to Jerusalem and Helsinki on fact-finding missions and to the Soviet Union to aid Refusniks (those Jews the Soviets refused to let emigrate). A board member of the Cleveland Anti-Defamation League until 1999 and formerly on ADL's National Legal Affairs and National Fact Finding Committees, he was active in ADL matters, including monitoring activities of hate groups.

Mr. Steinhouse, personally affected by the Holocaust, had lost family in German-occupied territory during World War II. He has published six books in his Holocaust series: *Wallenberg is Here!,*

Righteous and Courageous, Improbable Heroes, Barred, Wily Fox, and *We Shall Be Called Israel*. The books received rave reviews from Holocaust scholars and authors.

The author is happily married and lives in Naples, Florida, where he does his writing.

****

Joseph Richman is freelance feature writer and journalist. His works have been published in Florida and New York. He also interviewed TONY Award winner Henderson Forsyth for his role in the Broadway Show "The Best Little Whorehouse in Texas", which was published nationally in Soap Opera Digest.

Mr. Richman was a member of the Playwrights and Directors Unit of the Actors Studio in New York, under the late Harold Clurman and Lee Strasberg. Mr. Richman was also a member of the Playwright's Unit of the Neighborhood Playhouse (founded by Sanford Meisner) in New York. Mr. Richman studied screenwriting at the New School for Social Research in New York.

Mr. Richman developed screenplay for *The Outfielder* at the Actors Studio, under the leadership of the late Arthur Penn and Estelle Parsons and scenes were presented to the Studio Members, where they received positive reviews.